THE REWARD GAME

Imagine returning to your parked car and finding a corpse in it. This is exactly what happened to Molly Calder, and the discovery sparks the beginning of a tense trail for Molly and her husband Keith. They have their work cut out in chasing reward money for missing gems and missing money: the search leads them from their rural setting to the heart of Glasgow— and they need help from family and friends along the way. Molly wants to buy Briesland House more than anything in the world, although she's pretty keen on trying to keep her husband safe and sound—will she be successful?

THE REWARD GAME

Gerald Hammond

First published 1980
by
St. Martin's Press

This edition 2004 by BBC Audiobooks Ltd
published by arrangement with
the author

ISBN 1 4056 8502 6

British Library Cataloguing in Publication Data available

Printed and bound in Great Britain by
Antony Rowe Ltd., Chippenham, Wiltshire

Newton Lauder is a fictitious town in the general vicinity of Lauder and Newton St Boswells, or possibly Newton, Roxburgh. The story is even more fictitious. Most fictitious of all are the characters who, as far as I am aware, have no counterparts in real life.

G.H.

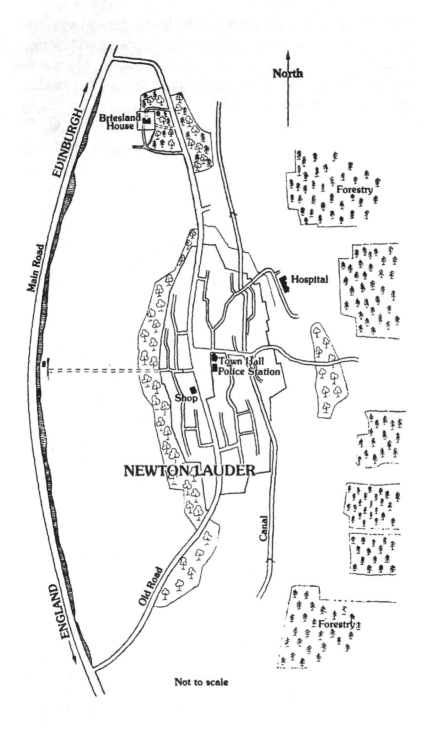

ONE

The shop had been shut for an hour or more but Keith Calder was still pottering among the guns and fishing-tackle. Outside, a golden spring sun shone low across the square of Newton Lauder, trying to chase away the memory of a bitter winter. Even in the middle of the small town there was bird-song. The birds were thinking of mating. Keith was thinking along similar lines.

But when Molly came into the shop, her husband put down the Franchi gun that he had been polishing, so quickly that he dented the barrel. And that was very unlike him; but Molly's usual happy grin was noticeably absent. She was white as paper and the whole of her small, plump self was shaken by regular tremors. Carefully controlling her hands, she unslung a camera with a large telephoto lens and set it gently on the counter. Then she fell into the customers' chair and put her head in her hands.

Keith had been relaxing over his labours with a glass of whisky at his elbow. He took the glass to Molly and raised her chin with one hand. Obediently, she sipped, while he held the glass.

'Are you all right?'

'I'll be fine in a minute. I've had a bit of a shock.'

'Is the car all right too?'

She lifted a hand and pushed the glass away. 'Keith Calder! Is that all you can find to ask – ?'

'I did ask first after you,' he said mildly.

'Yes. Sorry.' Molly took a few deep breaths. 'Bit of a

7

shock,' she said again. 'Car's all right. Except for a little blood.'

'Yours? You've got blood on your front.'

She looked down vaguely, and then shook her head so that her black hair swung across her cheeks. Her eyes looked large and unnaturally bright. 'Not mine, no. I think I'm all right now.'

Keith looked at her closely. 'You're not, but you'll have to do for the moment. Take your time and tell me what, for God's sake, happened. You went out to Bellcross Woods after that owl? Start from there and tell me all about it.'

'Well . . . I went out to the woods and settled down in my hide. Really, it's not so much a hide as a sort of nest scooped out in a gorse bush, and a bit of camouflage netting over it, and I settled down to wait.'

'He came?'

'Yes. I waited ages. I thought he'd come too late again after the light was gone. But then he came hunting down the ride, earlier than usual.' Molly lit up for a moment. 'I think I got a great picture of him stooping on a vole, but I won't know until I develop it. Then I heard a shot not very far off and I wondered if it was you. You sometimes go out that way.'

'Not me,' Keith said. 'You had the car, remember?'

'I've never known you be stuck. Anyway, I called but you didn't answer. The owl went off when he heard the shot, of course. I looked at my watch and it was getting late. I'd told you to put the potatoes on, but I knew you'd forget, so I decided not to wait.'

Keith's patience, never very great, was wearing away. 'But what was this shocking thing that happened? Come to the point before I burst.'

Molly looked at him with the hurt pathos of a whipped

puppy. 'I'm *coming* to that. I must tell it my own way. You said to start from the beginning and to take my own time. If you try to –'

'All right,' Keith said. 'All *right*.'

'But first I must go and have a pee.' She got up and scurried through to the small loo tucked away at the back of the shop.

Keith was left drumming his fingers on the counter. Then he laughed shortly, picked up the glass and drained it. The malt whisky was excellent, but it had never received the blessing of H.M. Customs and Excise.

'If you try to hurry me, you'll just make me flustered,' said Molly's voice, muffled by the door.

She came back presently and sat down. 'And then I'll forget something,' she said. 'Where was I?'

'Reciting all your reasons for coming home.'

'Oh. Yes. Well, I packed up my gear and set off back to the car along the ride. I could hear noises in the woods. I thought that old Donald's sheep had got in there again, but it sounded more like people.

'And when I got back to the car, somebody'd moved it. They'd turned it round and driven it about a hundred yards back towards the road, and the engine was running and there was a man sitting in it.'

'Hadn't you locked it?' Keith asked sharply.

'Yes, of course I had. But somebody's forced one of the quarter-lights. At least, the catch is broken now. But, Keith, how could they start the car without a key?'

Keith smiled at her innocence. 'That doesn't matter. Get me into almost any car and give me an ordinary penknife and I'll guarantee to start it within about fifteen seconds. What did the man have to say about it?'

'The man in the car?'

'Yes, the man in the car.'

9

'Nothing, Keith. He was dead.'

For a moment Keith felt reality slipping away from him. In his mind he sorted through several possible blasphemies that might have done justice to the situation, but in the end he decided that none of them would contribute much to the elucidation of the problem. 'And Tanya?' he said. 'What was she doing while all this was going on?'

'She was with me. She sits under the net as good as gold while I'm photographing.'

Keith paused. 'I suppose,' he said at last, 'that it's too much to hope that the gentleman was no more than a car-thief who'd popped off from a dicky heart in mid-theft?'

Molly shook her head again. 'He'd been shot. And he was sitting in the back seat.'

A lorry ground its way through the square, but it was very quiet in the shop.

'Bullet or shotgun?' Keith asked.

'Shotgun, it looked like.'

'All right. Let's go on from there. What did you do?'

'I didn't know *what* to do,' Molly said plaintively.

'I'm not sure that I'd've known either.'

'You'd have known, all right. You always do. What made it worse was that I'd seen him before. Do you remember the last time you went to Glasgow on business and I came along and we had lunch at that place in Nile Street?'

Keith stiffened. 'Of course.'

'Do you remember a wee chap, bald on top and a bit sweaty, who came and spoke to you, and you weren't pleased and you wouldn't tell me why?'

'Is that who it was?'

'Yes. And I didn't know what you'd want me to do. If you'd been up to something . . .'

'You didn't – ?' Keith found that his voice had gone up to a squeak, and he dragged it down by brute force and began again. 'You didn't think I'd shot him, did you? And put the body in our own car?'

'No,' Molly said doubtfully. 'But –'

'No buts. I don't get "up to" things. I never did, except maybe a little poaching.'

'And off-certificate guns,' Molly said.

'Well, yes.'

'And ammunition.'

'Yes, but –'

'And you did –'

'For Christ's sake,' Keith said, exasperated, 'stop cataloguing my past sins. I'm a strictly respectable shopkeeper and gunsmith now. I don't even poach any more. Not to call poaching.'

Molly looked away. 'I couldn't help wondering,' she said in a very small voice, 'whether he hadn't been wanting to talk to you about his wife or his daughter or something.'

'Good God!' Keith looked down at her, incredulously. 'You mean you thought I'd got into a quarrel with an angry husband or something?'

'Something like that.'

Keith pulled her to her feet and put his arms around her, but instead of melting she remained rigid. 'When we got married,' Keith said, 'I promised that those days were over.'

Molly sniffed. 'You didn't,' she said. 'Not quite. What you said was that you didn't make promises that you didn't mean to keep. And, Keith, I believe you. I believe you did mean to keep it at the time.'

'And I always have,' Keith stated. Certain trifling lapses, he felt, could well be ignored.

'Really?' Molly softened in his clasp. She sighed deeply.

In earlier days, Keith had been a rake with mistresses all over Scotland. Molly had known this and had still been happy to accept him in marriage because, loving him as she did, she could see that every other woman must love him too . . . 'Well, I couldn't be sure,' she said. 'It could even have been about some girl you knew before we were married. And there wasn't anywhere nearby that I could go to for help or to use a phone.'

Keith frowned. 'You must have been quite close to John Galloway's house,' he said.

'Was I? I didn't know.'

'No, you probably wouldn't. His drive comes off the side-road up to Donald's farm, and it bends round. His house is just beyond the crest at the end of the ride. But never mind that. What *did* you do?'

'What *would* I do? I pushed him down on the floor at the back, put your old mac on top of him and drove back here.'

'And told the police?'

'I thought I'd tell you first.'

Keith took several long, deep breaths and then said, 'Let's go and take a look.'

Outside, dusk was falling quickly. The street-lamps were alight, a mixture of comfortable old gas-lights and self-conscious new fluorescents so that the passer-by seemed to change in age and health in a few paces. The lamps hardly relieved the half-light, but Keith could see that apart from a motor-cycle leaning tiredly against the telephone-box in the corner of the square there was no vehicle to be seen.

Keith's capacity for rapid thought had kept him out of

trouble throughout most of a mis-spent youth. 'Which way was the car facing?'

'Back towards the north. I swung round the square so – '

'That's the way he's gone, then. I was facing the door all the time and he didn't go by. You're sure he was dead?'

'Positive. I've helped you gralloch enough deer to – '

'Was Tanya in the car?'

'Yes, I forgot to – '

'He's got a nerve, whoever he is,' Keith said. 'Crooks usually avoid cars with dogs in them.'

'Tanya wouldn't hurt a – '

'He wasn't to know that. Now, you run over to the police-station. Tell them, but give them the salient facts first. Tell them you found a body in our car but the car's gone, probably north. And tell them I've gone after it. And once they've got going on that, tell them the rest of the story.'

'But how are you – ?'

'I'll think of something. Go on. Scoot!'

Molly nodded briefly and scooted across the square to where the lights of the police-station shone beside the dark Town Hall. Keith watched her, torn between satisfaction that she could keep her head when lesser girls would have suffered hysteria, and irritation that her strict adherence to chronological order had wasted crucial time. When he was sure that she was out of vision, or at least too far away to argue, he sprinted over to the telephone-box.

The motor-bike was of an elderly model not unfamiliar to Keith, and the engine was still mildly warm. With a mental apology to its absent owner, Keith kicked it into life,

13

dropped it off its stand and set off with a swerve and a wobble.

The road northward out of Newton Lauder is an accelerated lesson in Scottish architectural history. Keith left behind the square where the baronial Town Hall and police-station face the Adam shop-fronts. Passing the early nineteenth-century shops and flats, Keith thought that he might live to regret his impulsive expedition. Where the late-Victorian villas gave way to early George V ribbon-development he was sure of it. And, as he left behind the last contemporary cedar bungalow and the last street-light, regret was already his dominant emotion. The night air was cold and he was not dressed for it. He was almost sure that he had left the shop unlocked. And he was on a fool's errand. In a very few miles the old road which had once carried the traffic between Edinburgh and the north of England would join the newer main road that bypassed Newton Lauder by the lip of the valley in which the old town lay. Probably his car, if it had ever left the town, had passed that junction by now, and it could have turned to any point of the compass, for in addition to the main road several lesser roads set off across the moors.

Darkness was closing fast and the motor-cycle's light was dim. Keith found his own car by nearly running into it. Another majestic wobble took him clear, and he dropped the motor-bike beside the road.

Keith ran to his car, heart in mouth.

His first concern was for his dog, and he called, 'Tanya!' To his infinite relief he heard a quick snort and saw the white patches of a liver-and-white spaniel appear and take up station beside his knee. He stopped for a moment and the bitch, just as relieved, pranced in front of him like some heraldic beast, rampant on a field sable.

The car seemed to lie canted with two wheels in the ditch. Keith's eyes were still only half-adjusted to the dark, but there was just enough light left in the sky to reflect in the car's panels, and the distorted reflections told of bodywork damage. Keith, whose insurance was as far from comprehensive as the law allowed, cursed silently.

The rear door resisted and then came open with a noise that combined a groan and a twang.

Keith was accustomed to handling birds and animals that had been shot or trapped so that a state of death held no dread for him, but he had to overcome a certain revulsion before he could bring himself to grope in the dark for a human corpse that might or might not be there.

It was there. Keith found it by putting his fingers into its mouth, and he nearly screamed. Pulling himself together, he brought himself to examine it by touch. The corpse was still warm and flaccid but the blood which had soaked its chest was crusting now. It had certainly been a 'wee chap, bald on top' once, but now it was, Keith told himself firmly, just a piece of meat. There seemed to be nothing in the pockets but the meanest and most easily recognised of trivia.

Tanya, who never barked, barked once, and Keith was aware of movement on the road behind him. He pulled back. As he straightened up, his world was shattered and filled with pain.

The climb back to consciousness was up a slippery ladder made of broken teeth that smelled of blood. Keith made it in a series of lurches, up the ladder and down the snake. Going up, his head hurt. Going down, his stomach heaved. Being conscious was the worst of all.

A flower-like pattern in the dark resolved itself into a ring of pale faces surmounting another ring of torches. The wet slapping at his face was Tanya's tongue. The softness under his head was Molly.

Keith spoke. The effort deserved to be rewarded by more than a feeble croak and a flash of pain. 'I don't think we closed the shop,' he said.

'I remembered,' said Molly's voice. 'I've been back.'

'Help me up.'

Her hands pressed his shoulders down. 'Stay where you are,' she said. 'There's an ambulance coming. You're going to the cottage hospital.'

Keith was going to protest, but he was sick instead all over a policeman's boots that smelled of polish. 'Come with me,' he said when the spasm was over. 'I want you with me.'

'Yes, of course.'

Keith looked up at the faces. 'And will somebody get that poor sod's bike back to him?' he asked. 'It was by the phone-box.'

Then the world faded away again.

TWO

Keith slept that night in a hard little bed in the cottage hospital. At first, between shock and drugs, he was deep in some secret limbo to which his consciousness could never return. Later, his sleep alternated between brief nightmares and periods of half-wakening to find that Molly was still beside him.

At dawn he woke fully at last. He tried to crawl back under the covers of sleep, away from the headache and the nausea, but the waking world refused to let him go. Molly was tipped forward across his legs, deeply asleep.

Keith lay quiet, trying to think of anything but how he felt.

At last the rhythm of Molly's breathing changed. She snorted once or twice, stirred and then sat up and blinked at him. Her hair, Keith thought, looked like unpruned clematis, but Molly looked better in the mornings than most girls did over dinner.

'Are you better?' she asked anxiously.

Keith could have discussed the subject at some length, but he had more urgent matters on his mind. 'Have you been here all night?' he asked.

She yawned, hugely. 'Most of it,' she said at last. 'It's all right, I won't leave you alone.' She patted his hand.

'Don't be a nitwit,' Keith said, 'and don't treat me as if I was an infant. The reason I asked is that I don't want you running around on your own.'

She stretched. It was a measure of his malaise that the spectacle did nothing for him. 'I only went home for a few minutes to feed Tanya and the ferrets. And myself,' she added as an afterthought. 'None of us had had last night's meal.'

Keith turned his head – slowly and carefully because sudden movements seemed to aggravate the nausea. He took hold of Molly's wrist. 'Look, I want you where I can be sure you're safe. There's something very odd going on and it's not finished yet. We've both been involved. Somebody might take that as a sign that we're connected with whatever-it-is in some way. So don't you go wandering off.'

'All right, dear,' Molly said.

Keith recognised the signs. When Molly spoke to him like that, she had not the least intention of paying more than lip-service to his demands. 'I mean it,' he said. 'This could be dangerous.'

They were interrupted by a harassed nurse who darted in and did things to Keith with a damp flannel. She tucked him in until his breathing was almost stopped and darted out again.

Keith struggled to win himself some breathing space. 'Why've I got a room to myself?' he asked. 'Am I in Intensive Care or something?'

'Nothing like that. I said you'd pay for the room.'

'Bloody extravagance!'

'I couldn't have stayed with you otherwise.'

They were silent for a minute. The sounds of dawn in a hospital filtered through the walls. 'Something seems to have happened to my face,' Keith said.

'I asked if you'd been kicked, but they said you'd fallen on it. They said you wouldn't be marked.'

'Nice to know I wasn't kicked,' Keith said. 'What happened after I wasn't kicked? No, go back further. What happened when you got to the police-station?'

Molly looked anxious. 'I was told if you woke up not to let you get excited. Should we be talking like this?'

Keith started to grit his teeth, but the shock-waves made his head pound. 'Listen, Fat Bum,' he said sternly, 'if you want to see me really excited just try not telling me what happened.' He shut his eyes and waited for her words to wash over him.

'Well,' Molly said. She paused. 'I went in and Sergeant Murchy was at the desk. You remember – ?'

'Yes, I remember Sergeant Murchy,' Keith said.

'All right. Anyway, he was very nice. He always is. I told him the first bit, just like you said, and he got on the radio at once and I heard him tell the two panda cars to go to the two places where our road joins the main road and to stop your car if it turned up. Then I started to tell him the rest of the story, but he sent for the . . . night-duty-inspector? Would that be right?'

'Probably.'

'So I told them both the whole story, and Sergeant Murchy got on the radio again and told them to stop every car going out and to look inside and into the boot. But he didn't say anything about a body.

'You hadn't come back, and the policemen in the panda cars hadn't seen your car go by. So the inspector sent for a car, then two constables came up from the canteen, and the inspector said I could go with them. And we were just going to leave when a phone-call came in from Mr Galloway at Briesland House, saying that your car was ditched near there. By Bellcross Woods where I was in the afternoon. So we got in the car and started off, and the inspector used the radio to call in the panda car from the other end to come along too. And there we found the car, and you doing your Sleeping Beauty bit beside it.'

'What about the body?'

'Not a sign of it, except for the blood. But you'd obviously been well clumped over the head, and what with that and the blood on the car seats I think they believed me. At least, I think they believed that I believed what I'd told them. But they maybe think that he wasn't really dead.'

'There was a dead body in our car all right,' Keith said.

'And our car has been tampered with, to run without the key,' said Molly, 'so they know that bit's true.'

Keith's head was swimming so he kept his eyes tightly shut, but there were things that he still wanted to know. 'They searched our car?' he asked.

'Oh yes. Thoroughly. But they didn't find anything interesting except the bloodstains.'

'I was wondering whether it was stolen for transport, or because something was hidden in it, or for the body. If the body's gone, it looks as if that was what they wanted.' Keith found that though his brain might be hurting it still worked. 'There didn't seem to be anything significant on the body, so maybe it was taken to hide its identity. Or perhaps somebody had taken whatever-it-was off the body before I got there. But in that case why take the body?'

'Don't ask me,' said Molly.

'Rhetorical question.'

'Well, don't ask me rhetorical questions I can't answer. The other man didn't have anything on him either. I heard one of the policemen say so.'

Keith opened his eyes again. 'Other man?'

'Yes. That was the next bit of the story. I knew I'd get muddled if you didn't let me tell it my own way.'

Keith sighed. 'Had you seen this one before?'

'I don't know. I didn't get to see him close to. It was when they were putting you into the ambulance. One of the men who were searching the surroundings found a man lying just inside the wood, about twenty yards from the car. He'd been bonked on the head too, but he was worse than you. I think he's been taken into Edinburgh for surgery.'

Keith slept again, unaware of the patter and bustle as the night staff were relieved. Next time he awoke, Molly had repaired her appearance and was toying with the remains of a meal on a tray.

'You've eaten my breakfast then?'

'Yes, of course. Did you want it?'

Keith considered the matter. 'God, no!'

'That's all right, then. Because they said you couldn't have any until the doctor's seen you.'

The doctor, when he arrived, came alone and looked as harassed as the nurse with the flannel. He was a thin, untidy man with a crop of dark, curly hair and a round blob of a nose. The label on his coat said 'Dr Watters'.

'Are you the vasectomy?' He looked vaguely at his clipboard.

'No I am not,' Keith said. 'You'd better get it right or I'll sue.'

The doctor turned over a page. 'No need to ask how you're feeling. Bloody-minded, right? You're not Mr Reynolds?'

'Calder,' Keith said.

'Is Gerry Reynolds having a vasectomy?' Molly asked. 'I wonder what he wants that for, at his age.'

Gerry Reynolds was a frequent customer, almost a friend, but he complained eternally about his purchases and was demanding of favours. 'Take them right off while you're about it,' Keith suggested.

Dr Watters looked even more harassed. 'Mr Reynolds isn't the vasectomy patient.' He flipped over another page. 'Calder? You're the concussion etcetera?'

'That's me all right,' Keith said.

'Any loss of memory?'

'None at all.'

'How's the appetite?'

'Yuck!'

'Well, at least you're predictable. Light hurt your eyes? Not much? Let's have a good look at you. You'd better wait outside, young lady. Pretty girl, your wife,' he added as the door closed behind Molly.

'You're not supposed to notice that sort of thing,' Keith said.

The doctor smiled faintly. 'We doctors are human too. Some more than others. We notice. It's just that we're not allowed to do anything about what we notice.' Suddenly the doctor threw off all signs of vagueness and Keith was subjected to a brief but searching examination, concentrating especially on his reflexes and ending with a careful study of his eyes by torchlight.

'What do you see in there?' Keith asked.

The doctor smiled again. 'I see you inside looking out.' He opened the door. 'All right, Mrs Calder You can come in again now.'

Molly, looking anxious in spite of her resolutions, scuttled back to her chair.

'The fact of the matter is,' said the doctor, 'that you've been clobbered, or in more technical language you've had a whack on the bonce. The X-rays we took last night don't show any skull damage, and the absence of amnesia is a good sign, but inside your skull your brain may have been bounced around like a pudding in a pan, if you'll forgive the analogy. I don't see any untoward signs and I don't expect to, but you'd better make up your mind to staying in here for a day or two.'

'I want out,' Keith said.

'You wouldn't make it as far as the door. I'd let you try for yourself, except that if there *is* any kind of damage you might aggravate it. You wouldn't be able to tell the difference lying down, but I'll be surprised if your sense of balance isn't a bit confused for a few hours yet. And I'm sending you into Edinburgh by ambulance. I'll make an appointment for you to get an E.E.G. at the Northern General.'

Molly turned white. 'Does that mean – ?'

'It doesn't mean a thing except that after a wallop like that and a dose of concussion like that and with a set of slowed-down reflexes like those it's only sensible to have a more direct study of the brain's workings. If they suspect anything, they'll keep him there; but if things are as normal as I believe, he'll be back tonight.'

'And out tomorrow?' Keith asked.

'If you're very good.'

'There's a policeman outside wanting to see him,' said Molly.

'No way!' said the doctor. He moved towards the door. 'I'll tell him to go and play with the traffic and come back tonight.'

'Before you go,' Keith said, 'can you tell me anything about the other chap who was brought in last night? Did you see him?'

The doctor sighed. 'Put it out of your mind,' he said. 'I'll tell you when to start worrying again, when you're fit enough. Until then, think calm and beautiful thoughts and try not to get excited.' He went out, and they heard his voice laying down the law to the waiting policeman.

'A medical comic!' Keith said disgustedly. He made

23

an effort to gather up the thoughts that were being pounded out of shape by a renewed headache. 'You'd better open up the shop. If Jimmy Smart comes in for his gun, give it to him and I'll send him in a bill. And John Galloway was probably trying to deliver that case of stuff last night. If you haven't heard from him by lunch-time give him a ring or go out there. But don't be alone. Have somebody with you all the time. Pay them if you have to, but don't be alone until we know what's been going on.'

'All right, dear,' Molly said.

'And if that bobby's still outside, tell him that I'll see him tonight, but that I can't add anything to your story except that the body really was dead, that it didn't seem to have anything interesting or valuable on it, and that if it's who you said it was it belonged to a little man called Chalmers, known as Noddy, who ran errands for a Glasgow dealer called Bruce.'

A nurse with a face of haunting innocence, but looking more harassed even than her colleagues, came in. 'Has the doctor been in here?'

'Dr Watters?' Molly said. 'He's been and gone.'

The nurse looked up at the ceiling for a moment. 'Oh Lord!' she said. 'It's Dr Beattie. Has he put Dr Watters' coat on again? No wonder he isn't answering his bleeper!' She slammed the door behind her.

Keith waited until the reverberations had stopped echoing around the remoter caverns of his head. 'And I'm supposed to be in here for peace and quiet!' he said disbelievingly. 'One thing before you go, Fat Bum. We're not involved in whatever-it-is, and we're not going to be. Right?'

'Right,' said Molly.

'All right, then. Give us a kiss.'

'You're not supposed to get excited.'

24

Keith dozed again on the trolley but awoke in the ambulance. A thin, surly-looking man whom he took to be the driver was looking down at him. 'And where might you be going?'

'The doctor said Northern General.'

'That's just great, that is. He told me City, but it says Western General on your slip.'

A stout man in hospital porter's uniform climbed in with them and sat down opposite Keith. 'What's he going for?' he asked.

'E.E.G.,' said the driver.

'That'll be the Royal Infirmary,' said the porter. 'Anyway, that's where I'm going so you may as well start there and see if he's expected.'

The driver grunted. 'That's if anyone's remembered to phone up about him at all. Bunch of clowns!'

'I don't know why they couldn't do it here,' Keith said irritably.

'You're joking,' said the fat porter. 'Last time they asked for a new enema tube it caused a panic in Admin. right up to Board level.'

For most of the way into Edinburgh Keith slept, and dreamlessly. When he awoke he still felt awful, but much less awful than before. He found that he could nod his head without sensing imminent disaster, so he nodded to the porter who was sitting hugging an attaché case on the other side of the ambulance.

'You're the mannie who got whacked on the nut last night, are you no'?' the porter said.

'That's me,' Keith said. 'One of them, anyway.'

'Aye.' The porter patted his case. 'I think I've a sample or two of yours in here among the suspected anaemias and a possible dose of the clap.'

'It's nice to feel wanted,' Keith said. 'Will you be coming back with me?'

'I'll be coming back with the ambulance. Whether you'll be with us, well, it all depends on what they find, don't it?'

'Would you like to do me a favour?'

The fat porter nodded. 'Sure. Just as long as it doesn't involve any cost, time or effort.'

'There was another man found near me last night. He was worse than me so he was brought into Edinburgh. Just as long as it doesn't involve any time, effort or expense, would you see if you can find out whether he's been identified yet and, if not, what he looks like?'

'I'll try,' the porter said. 'But, mind, I don't hold out much hope. Lots of hospitals in Edinburgh. Don't all do brains, though.'

A mile went by in silence. 'The suspected clap,' Keith said. 'It wouldn't be a Mr Reynolds, would it?'

'Couldn't tell you,' the porter said. 'The samples has only got numbers on them.'

'I see. It's just that my wife will want to know.' He was alluding to Molly's eternal curiosity, but the porter looked very oddly at him.

A telephone-call from the gate-house revealed that Keith was indeed expected at the Royal Infirmary, and he was trollied along the customary vistas of institutional corridors and endured the customary wait. The doctor was a silver-haired lady with a brisk manner and a sense of humour. She unwound Keith's bandages and admired the contusion.

'You wouldn't care to guess what it was done with?' Keith asked.

'You want my opinion as to the weapon? I'm not an expert, but I see a lot of this sort of thing in here. Something long, not a cosh or a hammer. Thicker than a poker, thinner than a rolling-pin – I see plenty of their work. Perhaps a crowbar, jack-handle, piece of lead pipe, something like that. And he hit you hard. He could have killed you.'

'Yes. The question is, did he?'

'Did he kill you?' She laughed. It sounded very young. 'I don't think so. If you were going to fall down with an intercranial haemorrhage you wouldn't be so chirpy just now – what is it? – sixteen hours or so after the event. But we'll just make sure that you're not going to develop a patchy memory or a stammer or something. Thank God they've shaved at least part of your head. It makes for good contacts and I shan't lose any of my terminals. Some of the hairy wonders I'm supposed to take readings off . . .'

Every time Keith was told to close his eyes he began to doze off, and whenever he was told to open them again he woke up feeling slightly better. He even began to flirt mildly with the doctor, but she told him to stop. It was not, she said, that she minded particularly; but she would be sending his traces back to Newton Lauder with her report, and she would not like them to go bearing her signature and such obvious indications of lust. Keith thought that she was probably pulling his leg.

Keith was returned to the ambulance at last, with an enevlope which, he was assured, contained nothing but good news. The stout porter was already waiting. 'You're in luck,' he said. 'I found your mate first go, through a pal of mine. He's still unidentified.'

'Did you get a good look at him?'

'Good as I could get with his head all wrapped up. Medium height, burly sort of build I'd say. My pal says he had brown hair, thinnish, cut short. He looked a bit of a tough to me.' The porter indulged in a good scratch while he thought over his description. 'Tell you what. Did you see a play on STV a couple of nights ago, the one about a robbery in a betting-shop?'

'Yes.'

'Remember the actor who played the manager? Dead image of him.'

'Well done,' Keith said. 'You're a pal!'

'Anything for a pal,' the man said complacently.

'Well,' Keith said, 'be a pal again.'

The porter nodded. 'Just as long –'

' – as it doesn't involve any cost or time or effort,' Keith said. 'That's understood. But you'll have to lend me the money. I've got money back at the hospital. There's something in it for you.'

'Like what?' the porter asked suspiciously.

'What I'd really like just now,' Keith said slowly, 'is a fish-and-chip supper and a pint of Guinness. If we're leaving Edinburgh by way of Gilmerton, there's a corner with a pub next to a chip-shop. If you got the driver to stop just round the corner . . .'

'It's against all the rules,' the porter said thoughtfully.

'And the same for yourself.'

'And the driver?'

'And the driver.'

'You're on. Coming into the pub?'

'In hospital pyjamas? You'll have to bring it out to me.'

'Can do.'

'Could you also find out for me what Gerry Reynolds is in the cottage hospital for?'

THREE

Back in his cold, hard bed in the cottage hospital, Keith did not seem to fancy even the meagre portion of fish and chips that was offered to him for his high tea. The staff were quite concerned. Molly arrived as his tray was removed.

Molly's cheeks were rosy and she brought with her the cold air of the world outside. 'Have I had a day!' she said. She dropped her woollen hat and her gloves on the bedside cabinet and bent down to give Keith a chilly kiss. 'The frost's setting in again. How did they say you were doing?'

'My brain's still in the right place, and I can go home tomorrow if I take it easy.'

'That's a bit quick, isn't it?' Molly said anxiously.

'These days you're lucky to come out of the anaesthetic and not find yourself sitting on your suitcase and leaning against the bus-stop. Help me up.'

'Are you supposed to be walking around?'

'Probably not, but I think it might help me to get over the wobbles.' He struggled to his feet and leaned on his wife. 'Now, let's do a few gentle circuits of the room. Did you find out what's wrong with Gerry Reynolds?'

Molly stopped suddenly, nearly throwing Keith off balance. 'How did you know I tried?'

'I could see that you were on the verge of bursting with curiosity, and I'd hate to have you explode. He's having his piles trimmed. Or he was. I think he got out today. Round we go. Whoops!' he added as his knees wobbled. 'Never mind. Tell me about the day.'

'Well . . . I went home and walked the dog and fed the animals, and then I got Minnie Pilrig to come in with me and I opened up the shop. There's a man wants to buy that Franchi shotgun, the over-and-under, but he's coming back to see you in a few days' time. A pair of guns were left for overhaul. A honeymoon couple came in and bought a lot of fishing-tackle, but I don't think they knew much about fishing; I had to tell them what they wanted. A carton of spinning-reels was delivered, and one of waders.'

Keith already knew that if she were speaking of an uneventful day that had culminated in an orgy of rapine Molly would still recount it in strictly chronological order. As usual, he could not resist making one attempt to obtain the information that he wanted in advance of the rest. 'Did you hear from John Galloway?' he asked.

'I'm *coming* to that,' Molly snapped. 'You're always so damned impatient. It's not as if you're going anywhere, and if I tell you out of order I'll miss something out. Several people rang up to ask after you. One of them, who sounded a bit Glasgow, wouldn't say who he was. And the clay-club secretary wants to place another bulk order. Then, just after twelve, Sir Peter came in.'

'Good,' Keith said. Sir Peter Hay, in addition to being their landlord and the local laird, was a friend, confidant, mentor and patron of the shop.

'He offered to look after the shop while we went to lunch.'

'You didn't let him, did you?' Keith asked anxiously.

'Good Lord no!' Molly said, laughing. 'I know how he fiddles around with things. He's like a bairn in a toy-box. I let him take me to lunch. We had –'

'I don't think I want to know,' Keith said quickly.

31

' – onion soup, a Dover sole, banana splits and that strong coffee with cream. It was lovely!'

'Help me back to bed,' Keith said. 'I'm feeling a little queasy again.' He got back between the stiff sheets and closed his eyes. 'But what about John Galloway?' he asked.

'Do you want me to go back to the beginning again?' Molly asked severely.

'For God's sake, no!'

'Well, I've just come to that bit, or I'd have to. And don't make faces. *Now!* I'd been phoning Mr Galloway's number all morning without getting an answer. And during lunch I mentioned this to Sir Peter. Keith, did you know that Briesland House belongs to Sir Peter?'

'I thought Galloway owned it.'

'Sir Peter said that Mr Galloway just rents it and he's giving it up. And, Keith – '

'You wondered whether we mightn't take it on?'

'Yes, that's right. And Sir Peter said that he didn't see why not. He hasn't found another tenant for it and he'd like to sell it. He said he'd give us a good mortgage deal.'

'He's been too good to us already,' Keith said.

'Well, let's not be too quick stopping him being too good to us again. Not until we have a proper home of our own. Anyway, I got Sir Peter to drive me out there. But it was all locked up tight, and Sir Peter said that Mr Galloway had paid off the couple who used to look after him. He knew, because they were taken on again by a friend of his. Sir Peter's, I mean.'

'Is Mrs Galloway still out in the Seychelles, or wherever it is?'

'I suppose so. Anyway, it was all locked up as I said. And it really is a lovely old place. Not *too* big, but lots of

32

room – we wouldn't be all cramped up as we are in the flat. But, Keith, it gave me a creepy feeling.'

Keith opened his eyes. He knew, or believed, that such 'feelings' were often the evidence of valid signals just below the level of conscious perception. 'What sort of "creepy feeling"?' he asked.

Molly pondered. Her frown of concentration was alien on her usually happy and carefree face. 'I think,' she said at last, 'that it was because there was so obviously nobody there except ourselves, and yet I felt watched.'

'But no sign of a watcher?'

Molly looked through him for a few seconds and then brought him into focus. 'I wouldn't say no sign at all. I thought I smelled tobacco. And just as we were leaving I thought I saw somebody's head over the boundary wall, out of the corner of my eye, but when I looked there was nobody there.'

'This was *after* you had the feeling of being watched?'

'Yes. And thinking about it, I thought that I remembered catching a glimpse of a car pulled into the wood near where the side-road branches off, so I looked on the way back but I couldn't see anything. Sir Peter said that I was imagining things, but I could see that he wasn't easy himself.'

Keith sighed. 'It's a worry, isn't it?' he said. 'I don't mind telling you that I've got an extra set of butterflies in the tummy. We borrowed a hell of a lot of money to buy that collection.'

Molly's eyes opened wide. 'Keith, you don't think he's taken the money and gone off, do you?'

'He's a man of substance,' Keith said slowly. 'A former M.P., vice-chairman of an insurance company, chairman of a company of developers, sits on God knows how many boards and committees.'

'So . . . ?'

'So he's just the type that gets itself into trouble, and I hope we haven't done the same,' Keith finished gloomily.

There was a silence.

'Maybe he's just gone away for a day or two,' Molly said hopefully. 'He missed us last night, and he'll get in touch when he gets back.'

'Maybe.'

'If it's just that . . . Keith, what do you think? Could we take on Briesland House? There's a lovely garden,' she added.

'So we'd need a gardener.'

'There's room for you to do professional dog-training again, to pay for the gardener.'

'Molly,' Keith said patiently, 'I'm already running a shop, working as a gunsmith and giving shotgun coaching in what little time I have left. Without waving my magic wand, I can't conjure up any more time. Briesland House has to be on or off by our present financial state. We'll have to balance our books, and see what kind of a deal we can get from Peter.'

'All right, dear, you wave your magic wand,' Molly said. She knew better than to press him when he was worried. Tomorrow would be another day.

They fell into a reverie, Molly thinking of her dream-house and Keith mentally balancing the firm's books and sending telepathic messages to the missing Mr Galloway.

Their silence was very thoroughly broken by the arrival of the police and the disturbance as extra chairs were fetched. Keith shut his eyes for one last doze through the hubbub. When he opened them again it was to find that he had been invaded, not by the entire strength of the Lothian and Borders Constabulary, but by two men. One, a fresh-faced constable with a parcel and a note-book, whom Keith remembered as a first-class trap-shooting competitor, could be discounted.

The other, unfortunately, could not. Keith and Chief Inspector Munro had long had a mutual respect based on complete antipathy. The chief inspector was a thin, dour-faced Hebridean who had risen in the police by virtue of great patience and a suspicious nature. He had an intense dislike of firearms of any kind in private hands, and Keith, as a stockist, purveyor and repairer of firearms, came in for more than his fair share of that dislike. Munro also considered – and not, on occasions, without justification – that Keith was inclined to treat the law with a respect that was, in Munro's view, less than its due.

'I'm sorry to see that you've been in the wars again, Mr Calder,' said the chief inspector.

Keith thought that the soft, West Highland accent was a poor medium for conveying sincerity. 'Thank you for your condolences,' he said. 'Where were you when it happened?'

Chief Inspector Munro looked at him austerely, but with the faintest gleam at the back of his dark eyes. 'If I had done that to you, Mr Calder,' he said, 'I would not be needing an alibi. Only an excuse.'

Keith told himself, not for the first time, that the pleasure of needling Munro was expensive in irksome and niggling persecutions, but it was a temptation that he could never resist. 'And what can I have the pleasure of refusing to do for you?'

'You can have the pleasure of telling me all about last night's events – all, that is, that you know of your own knowledge. I am not wanting a repetition of what you have heard from Mrs Calder here.'

Whatever their faults might be, Keith was an experienced witness and Munro a good listener, and it took only a few minutes for Keith's part in the previous night's alarms and excursions to be told and absorbed.

At the end, Munro was frowning. 'You're absolutely sure that he was dead? As sure as your wife is sure?'

'Surer than that,' Keith said. 'I've had more experience. When you touch a dead creature, if it's more than just a few seconds dead, you can tell. Not with a bird, maybe. You can't feel so much through the feathers, and sometimes they can fool you. But a shot rabbit, or hare, or a deer now. . . . For a minute or so, nerves are still jumping and muscles twitch, and I suppose there's still some blood circulating. Then, suddenly, nothing. Everything stops, the feel changes and the processes of decay begin. That's death, and you can feel it.'

'And that's how he felt?' Munro asked.

'That's just how. If I ever feel like that, you can bury me.'

'The chance would be a fine thing.' From an envelope, the chief inspector produced a small photograph and handed it to Molly with all the care and solemnity of a priest dispensing unleavened bread. 'Have you ever seen this man before?'

After only a glance, Molly nodded. 'That's the man I meant. The dead man.'

Keith received the photograph in turn and studied it. An affectionate message was scrawled across it, but he knew the face. It had belonged to a 'wee chap, bald on top and sweaty'. 'That's him. The man who spoke to me in Glasgow when Molly was there. Noddy Chalmers.'

'But you didn't see him, yesterday?'

'No. The interior light in our car popped last month and I never got around to fixing it. I was going to have it done at service. But by touch it could have been him.'

'And when he approached you in Glasgow, what did he want to talk about?'

'I don't know,' Keith said. 'I wouldn't listen to him.'

'And why would that be, now?'

'Because as far as I'm concerned his boss is bad news.'

Munro waited for the constable's pencil to stop moving. 'Go on,' he said.

'I just had reason to believe that he wasn't always scrupulous about the goods he handled.'

'What reason?'

'No very good reason,' Keith said, 'but enough. I bought several guns from Danny Bruce in the past, antique and modern. As far as I could tell they were perfectly legitimate. But I got whispers from friends in the trade, several different friends, that Bruce had been known to reset goods by passing them on to contacts in the trade. True or false, that was enough for me. In my business, any suspicion of dealing in stolen goods might give my good friend Chief Inspector Munro an excuse to interfere with my next licence application. So I stopped doing business with Bruce. And then I found out that he was still sending me things, using couriers like Noddy to front for him, posing as innocents wanting to sell Grandad's legacy. I still don't know that any of them were hot items, but I didn't feel very trusting. So I told Danny Bruce that anything else he sent me would go straight over to the police-station, and I was as surprised as hell when Noddy tried to contact me. I just gave him time to say that Bruce had sent him with a message and I told him, very nicely and politely, to go and bowl his hoop elsewhere.'

'Very virtuous,' said Munro. He stowed the photograph away in its envelope. 'Yes, it's Roderick Chalmers, known as "Noddy". After the information that you sent us last night, Glasgow got the photo from his fancy woman and sent it over this morning. Well, Mr Calder, that's all my questions for the moment . . . on that subject. I may want to speak to you again.'

'I shan't be far away,' Keith said. 'When can I get the car back?'

'Any time you like.'

'You've tested the blood on the seat?'

'Of course,' Munro said impatiently. He went on, after a moment's hesitation. 'Human. Group O.'

'Neither of us is O,' Molly said.

'I know that. We checked. Noddy Chalmers was O.'

'So,' Keith said, 'you have evidence accumulating, but no body? Right?'

'Quite correct. And, I may add, we've had a police car near each junction with the main road ever since you were found unconscious. If a body has left the district, I can't think how.'

'I wouldn't like to carry it out on my back,' Keith admitted thoughtfully. 'What about a horse?'

'I've had a word with the people at the riding-school.'

'Your men didn't look in my ambulance.'

'They did, you know,' Munro said with the pale shadow of a smile. 'You were asleep. My men thought they'd found the corpse.'

'What about the other man?' Keith asked. 'The one taken to Edinburgh. Has he been identified?'

'Not yet.'

'When Noddy Chalmers spoke to me, that day in Glasgow, another man was hovering nearby. I thought at the time that he seemed to be trying to hear what was said, although over the bar-chat noise he couldn't have made out a word. When Noddy left, the other man followed almost on his heels.

'While I was in Edinburgh yesterday, I asked the

38

hospital porter who rode in with me to see if he could get a look at the man you found near me, and from his description it was the man who was following Noddy around.'

'And Chalmers wasn't aware of the other man?'

'He gave no sign of it.'

'Very interesting,' Munro said flatly. 'Thank you for telling me. Now, there's one more thing.' He held out his hand and received the parcel which the constable had been nursing. 'This has been handed in to us. It is believed to have been found near the scene of your attack. It may have no connection with this case, but since it comes within what I am told is one of your fields of expertise I will ask you what you can tell me about this.' As he spoke, the chief inspector unwrapped the parcel, producing from the shrouding paper an antique pistol.

Keith took the weapon. There was an uneasy feeling in the pit of his stomach which was not the residual queasiness after his concussion, but habitual caution outweighed panic. He first borrowed a pencil from the constable and measured the length inside the barrel, comparing it with the external length from muzzle to touchhole. When he was sure that the pistol was unloaded he began a careful examination and, as he did so, he spoke absently to fill the silence. 'I always do that,' he said. 'Always. Muzzle-loaders are often still loaded when they turn up on the market, and accidents can happen even with a gun that was loaded a couple of hundred years ago. An empty gun wasn't much use, and the quickest way to clean them in the field, after firing, was to reload before corrosion set in. And once reloaded they were difficult to unload again except by firing them. Some men used to discharge them up the chimney when they got home, which also cleared the chimney of soot – and of the wife's boy-friend, if the old stories are true. So never handle one of these without making sure that it's empty.

'This is what's known as a Queen Anne or cannon-barrel pistol, but with a fixed instead of a turn-off barrel. Steel construction, walnut stock inlaid with silver wire, brass furniture. The lock is a normal flint sidelock, but of very high quality. It's a very good specimen by Walsingham, from about 1735. Very valuable. One of a pair. And,' he added grimly, 'it belongs to me. How did it turn up?'

For the first time, he had managed to surprise the chief inspector. 'Belongs to you? What way? Stolen from your shop, would you mean?'

'No, it never reached the shop. This pistol, or one remarkably like it, was in a collection that I bought from John Galloway. He was to keep them until my cheque cleared, and deliver them to me yesterday afternoon.'

Chief Inspector Munro's hesitation, this time, was more than a brief, contemplative pause. Keith could see that Munro was torn between conflicting courses of action. 'I think it only right to tell you,' Munro said at last, 'that Mr Galloway has been in Edinburgh since yesterday evening, giving the police help with enquiries which they are making into quite another matter. I cannot say any more, and ask you to keep the matter confidential. The information has not yet been released.'

'And nor has John Galloway?'

Munro ignored the question. He went straight on, in the precise lilt of one who learned to speak English by translating literally from the Gaelic. 'The pistol was found by a small boy. He took it home to play with. His parents thought that it was a toy. As soon as they realised that it was not, they brought it to us. The boy found it at the roadside, wrapped but not tied. He is not very certain as to the exact spot.'

Keith froze, staring stupidly into a corner of the ceiling. Molly waited expectantly, for this was Keith's expression when engaged in deep and urgent thought. After a few seconds Keith blinked. 'Two things, Chief Inspector,' he said. 'Firstly you'd better put the word about, in case any kids are running around with guns that haven't been unloaded. And, secondly, please give my wife help and protection to search for the others.'

'It'll be dark in a wee while,' Molly said.

'Never mind that. Get torches or something. Damn it,' Keith sat up, 'I'd better come with you.'

'*Oh* no, you don't,' said Molly, and Keith knew that when she spoke in just that tone of voice not even the Second Coming would change her mind. 'Here you stay until the doctors say that you can go.'

Keith lay back. 'Search the ditch and verges. Nobody would dump off one gun like that; they'd take the lot or nothing. Concentrate on the ditch on both sides of the road about fifty or sixty yards on from the place where I was skelped.'

'But – ' began Molly and Munro together.

'That's a prime collection,' Keith said. 'It took all our capital and we borrowed thousands on top. Molly, if we don't recover it, bang go your hopes of Briesland House! '

'Wouldn't it be better to wait until daylight?' Molly asked.

'Think, girl, think,' Keith said urgently. 'What kind of trouble would Galloway be in? A man like that, he's not inside for breaking and entering, or for slashing the seats in a football special. It just has to be fraud or corruption, something like that. His wife's abroad already. If he was just going to bugger off abroad and join her he could have

41

sold the collection several times over, to two or three other dealers. And whoever gets his hands on it first will have the strength of a completed deal to support him if there's a hassle in the courts.'

'All right,' said Molly. 'I'll wave my magic wand.'

'Girls don't *have* magic wands,' Keith said. He turned over and punched his pillow.

After a somnolent day, Keith was now wide awake and twitching. He lay for nearly two hours trying not to bite his fingernails before a night-nurse, a plain girl but with a figure that Keith considered to be gorgeous, came in.

'Your wife's on the phone,' she said. 'I'm to tell you that they've recovered all but two, whatever that means.'

'Which – ? Never mind,' Keith said. 'I'll come through and speak to her. Let me lean on you.'

She let Keith lean on her. Keith's sense of balance had come back, but so had his other senses. He had never missed a chance to get an arm around a gorgeous figure. It may be that there is no prude like a reformed rake, but Keith did not consider himself to be quite as reformed as all that.

In the small office, Keith sat on the desk and picked up the phone. 'What's missing?' he asked Molly.

Molly sounded tired. 'Sorry I took so long, but I was checking against your copy of the list,' she said. 'They all match up. We're short of one Tower pistol with nipple-barrel conversion, and also the last one on the list, the tap-action boxlock.'

'Well done, Fat Bum,' Keith said. The nurse gave a muffled gasp. 'You've got all the valuable stuff. Stow it away safely and I'll thank you properly in the morning. Was one of them just beside where our car was stopped?'

'That's right. In the ditch.' Molly put surprise into her voice. She had come to expect Keith to pull rabbits out of hats, but it did him good to be admired now and again. 'How did you know?'

'Somebody forced our car into the ditch. He would have come to a halt further along. I didn't see his vehicle by the light on that motor-bike, so I made a guess at fifty yards. Right? Then he came back and whacked the driver – possibly vice versa, but I don't think so. D'you follow me?'

'Yes,' Molly said doubtfully.

'Right,' Keith spoke slowly, thinking it out as he went along. 'Then he hauled the other man into the wood. He wanted to make off with the body. He wanted something to put the body in, probably to keep blood off his own car. For some reason the case of guns was handy, so either it was John Galloway doing all this or somebody was using his car. Or don't I remember Mr G. with a Land Rover?'

'You do,' Molly said.

'The perfect vehicle to push our car off the road with, and his house was nearby. Let's assume that he went back to the Land Rover, emptied the guns into the ditch and that's about when I arrived.'

'So the holster pistol where our car was ditched – '

'Was what he used to thwack me with. Exactly. It fits, doesn't it?'

'Where it touches,' Molly said.

'If it was John Galloway doing all that, he knows where the body is. Could you get onto Munro, or somebody else if he's off duty, and suggest tactfully that they try to get it out of our friend, and also that they question anybody who tries to get in from outside to see him?'

'I'll do that.'

'Did Munro let on what our friend's inside for?'

43

Molly's chuckle came over the wire, and for a moment Keith could see her laughing. 'Not Munro,' she said. 'He wouldn't tell you the way across the street. But he sent Sergeant Murchy out with me. Mr Galloway's being questioned by the Big Deal Mob, or whatever you call it.'

'The Serious Crime Squad?'

'I think so. Anyway, it's about fraud and it's very big. I'd never have believed it of him.'

'Poor sod!' Keith said. 'How are the mighty fallen! Well, none of it's any skin off our noses, thank God! Is that the lot?'

'That's the lot. Good night, darling.'

'Love you too, Fat Bum.'

Although the nurse was eaten with curiosity, she was less happy to be leaned on, going back.

FOUR

In the morning the real Dr Watters not only pronounced Keith fit to go home but managed to convince an anxious Molly that, provided that he took it easy and kept his head out of the way of blunt instruments, he would be none the worse. They emerged at the top of the hospital steps into bright sun and a bitter chill.

'I'd better drive,' Molly said. 'The car must have sat down on something. It's like trying to steer a camel by the tail, but I've got sort of used to it. The police only let me take it away because I was going straight to a garage.'

'But you weren't,' Keith pointed out.

'So I lied. But I am now.'

The car groaned as it moved. 'It sounds like I felt yesterday,' Keith said.

'You're sure you're all right now?'

'I feel like two tons of dynamite.'

'Then that's what you shall have.'

As they turned out of the hospital gates the town was laid out below, needle-sharp in the frosty air, a jumble of grey roofs and smoking chimneys with trees standing, apparently through the roofs, like fixed explosions. Beyond, the ground rose again from the valley of the town, at first gradually in a quiltwork of agricultural land and then, where Gerry Reynolds' cottage blinked white in the sun, the hill rose sharply to the main road. When they stopped, the noise of the traffic came clearly across the valley.

At Ledbetter's garage, the proprietor came out of his

wooden office to meet them. Keith ducked cautiously out of the car. Mr Ledbetter looked at the bodywork damage and tutted. Then he looked under the car and tutted some more. 'It'll take a while,' he said.

'How long?'

'Parts are slow, after the strike.'

'How long?'

'I can try the agents, of course.'

'How long? You're as bad as Molly,' Keith added.

'Six weeks. M'hm.'

Keith groaned. 'We can't manage without transport for as long as that. Got anything you could hire us?'

'Sorry. Hired.'

'Both of them?'

Mr Ledbetter nodded his head. 'Both taken yesterday. One by a honeymoon couple, staying at the Royal. And the other by a couple of men, toughs if you ask me. I think they're staying at the Black Cock. So there you are.'

'Come on, Mr Ledbetter,' Molly said. 'You've never let us down yet. There must be *something*.'

'There's a wee sports car that I took as a trade-in, but it's not what I'd call a business vehicle.'

'Not unless you were selling it,' Keith said. 'Well, just as long as it's wheels.'

Keith went into the office and signed papers. Molly put down the roof of the little red car and dumped herself firmly in the driving-seat before Keith came back.

They buzzed happily back to the shop. The cold air made their eyes water. As they pulled up outside the shop a white car overtook them. 'Isn't that one of Mr Ledbetter's cars?' Molly asked.

'I think so.'

'It's been in and out of the driving mirror all morning.'

46

Keith opened the shop while Molly went up to the flat to finish the housework. He was hardly in at the door before the phone rang. He picked it up.

The voice that spoke in his ear was a man's, but high-pitched and fluting. The accent was Glasgow but mild, Bearsden rather than Cowcaddens. 'Listen, Calder,' it said. 'You know where it is and we're coming to collect it. Better let us have it without any trouble.' Then the connection was broken.

Abstractedly, Keith moved towards his workshop. Then, on a thought, he darted back to the shop-window and looked out. But if the call had been made from the call-box across the square he was too late. He tried to remember whether he had heard coins drop.

Keith shrugged and went into the workshop. When Molly came down he had a pair of old Damascus barrels on the bench and was polishing them to silver with the finest of emery cloths.

Molly dumped a tray of coffee and biscuits on the bench. 'Are those the barrels from that gun of Lord Fowler's?'

'Yep.'

'You've knackered them, haven't you?'

'They were knackered before,' Keith said patiently, 'by years of bad use and neglect. Now I've got to start again.'

'My mistake,' Molly said. They exchanged a grin. It was good to be back. But not perfect.

'I had an odd phone-call just now,' Keith said.

'You've got it, we want it?'

'Something like that. You've had one too?'

'On the house phone, before I left to fetch you. I wasn't going to mention it until you were better.'

47

'I'm better. Well, I can't say I'm all that surprised. Somebody wants something, as I said. And it seems that he hasn't got it. And we've been turning up wherever anything odd was happening. That's why I didn't want you to be alone.'

'I notice that you didn't come upstairs with me.'

'I'm too much of a coward,' Keith said. 'I thought that they were waiting for us upstairs.'

Molly leaned against his back. He could feel her laughing. 'Whatever you are, you're not a coward,' she said. 'You just forgot, didn't you?'

'All right, I just forgot. If I forget again, remind me. Did you tell the police about the phone-call?'

'Yes, of course.'

'Well, from now on I'll answer the phone. If it rings while I'm out don't answer it.'

'They can't hurt me over the phone,' Molly pointed out. 'And we can't afford to lose business.'

'Not if you're going on a spending spree,' Keith agreed. He fitted wooden plugs into the muzzles and breeches of the barrels and started to de-grease them with limewater.

'Take your coffee,' Molly said. 'Then shall we go and look at Briesland House?'

'We'll take an early lunch-hour. As you said, we can't afford to turn away business.'

'Not if I'm going on a spending spree. Keith . . . Those phone-calls. Were they talking about the body?'

'It sounds likely.'

Molly shivered. She flopped into the comfortable, broken-down old armchair beside the work-bench. 'Keith, why would anybody want the body? You said that there wasn't anything on him.'

'Nothing to do with us,' Keith said. He decanted Greener's Solution into a glass bowl.

'All the same, *why?*'

Keith spoke slowly. He began sponging solution onto the barrels. 'I didn't check him to see if he was carrying what they call a "charger". I could have missed a slip of paper carrying a map showing where the treasure's buried. Or for the matter of that, he could have a secret formula tattooed between his shoulder-blades. Or – '

The shop door-bell rang, and Molly went through to serve. She came back with a sheath-knife. 'The tag's missing off this. How much is it?'

Keith glanced up. 'Twenty-two quid.'

'I can't ask *that*! Just for a knife!'

'That's the price. There are cheaper ones. But never suggest to a customer that he can't afford what he wants.'

Molly went back into the shop and Keith worked on with his sponge. The till rang, then the door-bell. Molly came back, her eyebrows up to her black fringe, and dropped into the armchair. 'He paid it,' she said. 'Twenty-two pounds for a knife!'

Keith shrugged. 'If you want the very best, you can pay a lot more than that.'

Molly looked at her watch. 'Can't we go out to Briesland House now?' she asked.

'Business first, houses later.'

'All right. Go on about what they might have wanted the body for.'

'Mm? Oh, yes. Well . . . it could be as simple as that somebody has to keep the body out of police hands because, say, his fingerprints would connect him with another crime which would land his associates in the cart. Or maybe there was a contract on him, and proof of his death was required. Or – I dunno – perhaps they were going to sell his body to medical science.'

Molly reached out and kicked him gently. 'Be serious.'

'It's got nothing to do with us, and I hope it stays like that. Why should I waste my precious mental energy solving hypothetical problems with inadequate data?'

'Because you love me.' The door-bell rang. 'Damn! Never mind. A few more of those knives and we'll be able to afford Briesland House.'

She came back in two minutes and looked over Keith's shoulder, nudging him deliberately with her breasts. 'Packet of fish-hooks,' she said disgustedly. 'Hullo! The pattern's coming back already. Laminette, right?'

'You're learning. You know,' Keith said, 'they might want to have him stuffed and stand him in the corner as a hat-rack.'

'Don't be gruesome. Keith, do we give a taxidermy service? Somebody was asking.'

'Yes. I send them in to Edinburgh. You know, probably they just wanted the body to get rid of it, to cover up the fact that they shot him.'

'Then who's got the body, if it isn't themselves?'

'Probably another branch of the same gang.'

Molly laughed. 'I thought only big business made that sort of a boo-boo.'

'Gangs *are* big business.'

The bell pinged again and Molly got to her feet. 'This one's going to buy a knife whether he wants it or not,' she said. But she came back immediately with a visitor.

Keith looked up. 'Why, hullo! It's Mr . . . Gulliver, isn't it?'

The newcomer, a man in his early fifties, presented an

image that was both neat and elegant. His grey hair was carefully trimmed and brushed, his clothes seemed casual but were well cut and looked brand-new, and his face and carriage suggested generations of breeding. He might well have been a diplomat. He was, in fact, the chief investigator for a major group of insurance companies.

Keith wiped off Lord Fowler's barrels and put them aside. 'Nice to see you again,' he said. He genuinely liked Andrew Gulliver. 'I've hardly seen you since your enquiries into my van that blew up.'

Gulliver smiled. 'You got the cheque in the end? That's good. Of course, we met again on that shoot at Dumfries, but we didn't have much time for a chat.'

Keith waved him to a seat in the armchair, and Molly perched up on the bench. 'What brings you into this backwater?' Keith asked. 'It can't be the new dent in my car, because I haven't had time to make out a claim and they wouldn't have sent a big wheel like you anyway.'

'Not a sparrow shall fall,' Gulliver said. 'You mean the car that was stolen the night before last and run off the road?'

Keith kept his face blank. 'I always suspected that you did your investigating with the aid of a competent clairvoyant and a cup of tea-leaves,' he said lightly.

'Nothing occult about it,' Gulliver said. 'I was with an old friend of yours in Edinburgh this morning and he told me all about it. You remember Superintendent Gilchrist?'

Keith frowned. 'I thought he was with Strathclyde.'

'He is. But they have an interest in the matter that brought me down here. He thinks very highly of you, by the way. It seems that you did him a favour once. Anyway, he grinned all over his face and said that I should come and see you. What would that be about, would you know?'

'At a guess . . . are you interested in John Galloway and his little bit of trouble?'

'Very much.'

'That would be it, then.'

'Unless,' said Gulliver, 'you know something about a parcel of gems that went missing from Prestwick Airport last month? Or attempted arson at Grangemouth?'

'Not guilty,' Keith said.

'Well, keep your ears open. I seem to remember that they heard most of what went on. There's a ten per cent reward for the gems, by the way, and the sum involved would curl your hair. Usual conditions. Now, do you know something that I don't about John Galloway and his "little bit of trouble"?'

Keith started to tidy his bench. 'Probably,' he said. 'First you tell us about it.'

Gulliver raised his eyebrows and then laughed. 'He was charged this morning and it will be all over tomorrow's papers, so I suppose I could. We've just uncovered a major fraud. A very clever one, too, and very hard to detect because it was covered up in the transferring of under-writing risks between two of our companies that are audited separately. It had been going on for years, and it might have gone on indefinitely but for an accountant leaving one company and joining the other and then happening to notice a discrepancy. Like a sensible chap he came to us instead of to his bosses. But somebody gave something away. Suddenly, before we could act, they were running. One of the conspirators got out of the country, we caught one on his way to the airport, another one has disappeared and some smaller fry stayed at work and tried to bluff it out. But John Galloway was the brains of the operation and we were lucky to get him. He had an air ticket on him for Algiers, but he was already too late to catch the plane.'

'How much is missing?'

'We shan't know until we've done a complete audit, if then. Insurance risk-money isn't like other profit-and-loss accounting. But it looks like upwards of a couple of million. Frankly, we'll get a quicker and more accurate picture by examining the personal accounts of Galloway and his friends. However much it may prove to be,' Gulliver pulled a face and then shrugged, 'I suppose Mrs Galloway is incubating a large part of it.'

'In the Seychelles?'

'No. If she were in the Seychelles we could get her back. Now, what can you tell me?'

So Keith and Molly, between them, told the story of their slender acquaintanceship with Galloway and his status as an occasional customer, the purchase of the gun-collection and its non-delivery, the body, the theft of the car, the nobbling of Keith and the mysterious appearance of the guns. Keith repeated the reconstruction of events that he had outlined to Molly.

When they had finished, Gulliver was looking puzzled. 'I can't understand why Gilchrist referred me to you,' he said. 'Unless he knows something that we don't, your part in the affair would appear to have been both peripheral and transient. It does seem quite possible that Galloway was involved in the shooting of this man and in the recovery and disposal of the body. We don't know yet, and, understandably, Galloway is confining his remarks to irrelevancies and saying precious little about those. In his place, I'd do the same. It is even possible that you do know something that would help, without even realising that you know it. But just how the hell Gilchrist would know or even guess that you might know it is beyond me. There must be a Glasgow connection that we don't even know about.'

'Beats me,' said Keith.

'Obviously Galloway knew that the cat was about to escape the bag. He bundled his wife abroad with most of the proceeds, and remained behind to dispose of the more valuable property such as the gun collection, hoping to be out of the country before the axe fell. Then his arrangements got loused up by the killing, he missed his plane and fell into the hands of the police.'

'When – ?' Molly began. She stopped.

'Yes?'

'Just a thought. But when did you first know that there had been a fraud?'

'Exactly a week ago today,' said Gulliver.

'Then she didn't take anything with her,' said Molly. 'She flew out a week ago last Wednesday, and she'd been planning her trip for a month before that.'

Gulliver broke a short silence, rubbing his hands together. 'There's been no indications so far that Galloway had been sending money abroad as fast as he collected it. So there's a chance that the bulk of his share is still in the country, I'm very much obliged to you, Mrs Calder.'

'I haven't changed anything,' Molly said.

'Ah, but you've given me the precious gift of hope.'

'Do you happen to know how and where they caught him?' Keith asked.

'Generally, yes. Police from Edinburgh went to Briesland House the night before last, round about the time that you were being clobbered. They found the house apparently deserted. Having the necessary warrant they entered the house, no doubt after a discreet interval, leaving an inconspicuous guard on the front door. And the next thing they knew, he'd walked in on them through

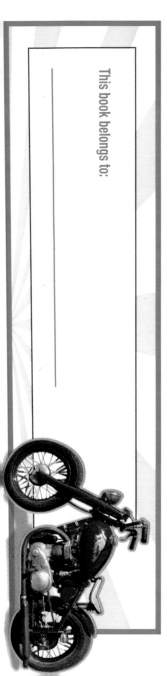

This book belongs to:

the back door. I believe that the first they knew of him was when they heard somebody speaking on the kitchen extension. The inspector who was in charge of the party got a good chewing-off for his carelessness, but all's well that ends well.'

'I see,' Keith said. He stared vaguely into the air, somewhere behind Gulliver's shoulder.

'Well,' Gulliver said briskly. 'I'll be staying at the Royal for the next few days, since this is where most of the action seems to be. Get in touch if you think of anything. Perhaps you'd like to dine, both of you. I'll ring you.'

'We'd love to,' said Molly. She nudged Keith.

Keith came back to life. 'We've got a lot of pigeon around here,' he said. 'Would you care for an hour or two's decoying? Or a roost shoot?'

'Love it. And now I'll leave you to get on with your business. Perhaps Mrs Calder would come through with me. There are one or two things I want.'

It was some minutes before Molly came back, and then she was beaming. 'He said he already had one of those knives. But he bought a whole load of other stuff. Oh, sorry!' she added.

Keith came back out of his reverie. He blinked and stretched. 'If we're doing so well, you can give me one of those knives for my birthday.'

'I can't afford our prices.'

'I'll give you a fat discount.'

'We are not giving discounts any more,' Molly said firmly. 'And why do you want one, anyway?'

'I'll tell you. I saw a Norwegian with one of them last year. He was a deck-hand on a trawler that was in Eyemouth. She was moored with wire hausers, and they'd left it a bit late as the tide fell. He made everyone stand well back, and then he slashed the hawser with his knife.

55

The trawler dropped about a foot. But the point is that you could still have shaved with the knife afterwards. Well, not you, but I could have. That's when I decided to stock them. But never mind that just now. I'll persuade you when we get upstairs tonight.'

'Oh, you will, will you?' Molly put her tongue out at him.

'With pleasure, as they say. But,' Keith said seriously, 'I had an inspiration and you blew it away. I've got some of it, but I lost hold of the rest. It'll come back.' He got up off his stool. 'Here a minute.'

In the strong-room Keith pointed to the rows of bundles where Molly had laid out the collection of pistols on the shelves. 'You found one near where our car was ditched and the rest further up the road. Right?'

'Right,' said Molly.

'Do you know which one was the one on its own?'

'That's easy,' Molly said. She picked up a parcel wrapped in yellow plastic. 'It was unwrapped, so I found an old fertiliser bag.'

Keith opened the parcel and took out a heavy flintlock pistol. He examined it carefully under the strong-room lamp from all angles. 'I thought so,' he said. 'I bloody *thought* so.'

'What?' Molly said. 'What did you think?'

'I think that we want that body. I think that we want it very much indeed.'

'You speak for yourself,' Molly said. 'If there's anything I want less, I can't think what it is.'

Keith laughed. 'Yes you do. You don't know it yet, but you want it all right. Oh well, let's go out to Briesland House now, shall we?'

'When I say that, you don't listen,' Molly said. 'Come on, then. What are you doing?'

56

Keith had taken down a box from the top shelf and was unwrapping a Ruger automatic pistol. 'I'm tying a knot in my leg,' he said. 'What do you think I'm doing?'

'No guns,' Molly said firmly.

'It's time we were armed. You too, if you like.'

'Keith, we're not licensed to carry firearms, only to deal in them from the shop. Munro could put us out of business. Anyway, we're only going out to look at a house.'

'Other people might not know that,' Keith suggested.

'You've always been able to look after yourself in a scrap, and after me too. But if you carry a gun, first thing you know somebody else with a gun might feel that he had to use it. Keith, *please*.'

Keith saw that she was near to tears. 'Well, all right,' he said reluctantly. 'But it's against my better judgement. I hope we don't live to regret it. Or rather, I hope we do live to not regret it.'

'You can always wave your magic wand,' Molly said.

FIVE

Now that Keith wanted to leave for Briesland House, circumstances seemed determined to delay his departure.

First, he cleaned the pistol that had been in the fertiliser bag, for fear that the chemicals might be corrosive. That delay enabled a smiling constable to intercept him at the door, carrying a tiny boxlock pistol and a receipt on which he wanted Keith's signature.

'A lady brought this one in,' he said. 'She was up to high do. She found her nephew playing with it, and she knew that it didn't belong to her sister's family. She took it home, thinking that it was one of those cigarette lighters. And when she tried it out she put a ball through the front of the television. She said she was going to sue you.'

'She'll be lucky!' Keith said. 'The old bag was going to keep it.'

'Aye. That's what the sergeant said, and he told her that she could be had up for the reckless discharge of firearms. I doubt you'll hear any more from that quarter. This is one of yours?'

'No doubt of it.' Keith showed him the entry in the list, and they compared the maker's name.

The constable picked up his receipt. 'Well, that's it. One to go.'

Keith watched the blue back retreating out of the door. 'Two,' he said softly to himself. 'Two to go.'

This time they got as far as the pavement outside the shop. A very battered old Land Rover pulled up beside them and Gerry Reynolds' bald and wrinkled head popped out, tortoise-like on a long neck. His usual big grin was missing.

'See you a moment, Keith?'

'Surely,' Keith said, hiding his impatience. 'Molly, love, would you pop up and bring Tanya down while I talk to Gerry?'

Molly nodded and trotted off. Although she tried to keep it a secret it was common knowledge that she still adored her husband, and if from time to time he treated her as if she was a favoured spaniel she would generally react with spaniel-like docility.

In contrast to Andrew Gulliver, who was an investigator but looked like a diplomat, Gerry Reynolds was a retired diplomat who could have passed himself off as anything from a low-class private eye to a tramp. He had taken an early retirement and returned to his native area. He had knocked together the two cottages on the hill to make a comfortable bachelor home, and was passing a long retirement by paying a small rent for the shooting rights of the farmland around his cottage and acting as his own gamekeeper. After years of work for which sartorial elegance was obligatory, he now cultivated a dedicated scruffiness at all times except on shooting days when he emerged in magnificent tweeds and an aroma of mothballs.

'What can I do for you?' Keith asked.

'A favour, I hope.'

Keith tried to smile. Reynolds was a demanding customer and, although he was good for the occasional shooting invitation, he was an ungenerous host when the time came to share out the bag. But, Keith thought, it might be quicker to agree than to argue. 'What favour?' he asked.

'I'm staying at the Black Cock for a few days. Don't feel

much like walking.' Reynolds' appearance might no longer suggest the Diplomatic Corps, but he still sounded Herriot's-and-Oxford.

'I bet you don't,' Keith said.

'You know then, do you?' Reynolds leaned further out and lowered his voice. 'It's the stubble, you know. They shave you, of course, and while it's growing back the stubble makes walking bloody murder. I can't get the Land Rover all the way up to my place, and I'm damned if I'm walking it just now.'

'You want me to go up and fetch something for you?'

'No, no. I've got all I need. It's my pheasants. I've got a good wild stock, and they'll soon be getting ready to nest. I left them plenty of food in the hoppers, and water as well. But if this frost gets any worse they won't have any water. They'll wander over onto Sir Peter's shoot, and they won't come back.'

'All right,' Keith said, 'if the frost persists I'll go up and water them tomorrow. Is it all right if I shoot a few pigeon?'

'Of course. Just try not to disturb the game-birds.' Reynolds took up a few more minutes in explaining where his feed-hoppers were placed that year and where the key of the cottage was hidden, and then drove off with no more than a brief nod of thanks.

Tanya was fussing around Keith's feet, delighted to see him again after a separation that had lasted for nearly two hours. 'If we get any free time, maybe we'll go after the woodies,' he told her as he pulled her ears.

Molly, meantime, had deposited herself in the driving-seat of the little sports-car, but Keith was insistent that it was his turn to drive. Grumbling, Molly got out and walked round the car.

Keith had forgotten what it was like to drive a small,

responsive car, open to the wind and with a girl at his side. He enjoyed the two-mile run out to Bellcross Woods, but not so much that he forgot to watch the mirror. As far as he could tell they were not followed.

Just short of the woods he turned left onto a narrow tarmac road that served a farm and a small market-garden. The woods gave way to a stone wall and Keith turned in through the gates of Briesland House. The drive ran uphill, so that when Keith had made a semi-circle on the gravel apron and parked facing south again they were looking over the wall and away down the valley to the town.

'Nice,' Keith said.

'It is a lovely house, isn't it?' Molly said, twisting her head round.

'I meant the car. We need a second vehicle.'

Molly's voice was raised in indignation. 'Keith Calder! You are such a bastard I don't believe your mother even *met* your father! I bring you out here to look at a house, and you want to spend precious money on a sports-car!'

Keith knew that as long as he didn't laugh he could persuade Molly to agree to anything in the end. 'We'd save money,' he said, 'if we didn't have to use a lumbering, greedy monster of an estate-car even for one-person no-luggage trips, and do extra journeys fetching each other because we both depend on it. And think of all the extra commuting between here and the shop.'

'If and when we get this house,' Molly said, 'then we may just start to think about a second car if and when we can afford it.'

'If and when we get out of the car we might just start to take a look around.'

They left Tanya in the car and walked round the house, peering in at windows.

'They're nice, sunny rooms,' Molly said suddenly, 'and

61

they need hardly any redecorating. What do you think?'

'I wasn't looking at the rooms.'

'What, then?'

'I was looking for an old, tin trunk.'

Molly sighed in exasperation. 'What for?'

'The tin trunk the guns were in, last time I saw them.'

'If he wants a tin trunk then he shall *have* a tin trunk,' Molly said. 'Then maybe I can get some attention.' She led Keith round another corner, to a yard that was enclosed on three sides by the house and outbuildings. There on the cobbles stood an old, tin trunk. 'Never say again that girls don't have magic wands,' she said.

Keith looked around. On one side of the yard was the back wall of the house and a door into the kitchen quarters. The wall opposite was blank, and Keith guessed that it was the back wall of some former stables. A plum-tree and a pear were neatly trained over its whitewash. The third side of the yard was taken up by what Keith could see, by peering through dirty glass, had been a wash-house.

Molly waited while Keith stared sightlessly at nothing. She hoped, without very much confidence, that he was giving his mind to such problems as mortgages, central heating and new curtains.

'Wash-house!' Keith said suddenly. 'Of course! That's exactly what I'd have done.' He examined the door. It was locked, but a small pane was missing beside the lock and the key was inside. Keith put his hand in through the hole, but the position was awkward and the lock was stiff. He took the key out and inserted it from the outside. The lock groaned and the key turned.

'Keith,' Molly said. She swallowed. 'Keith, we wouldn't really be looking for the body, would we?'

'Yes, of course we are.' He pushed the door open. The

gloomy interior was filthy. Evidently the place had been used for years as a gardener's stores, and the floor was scattered with dried earth, but the two original sinks loomed, large and white, on the opposite wall, and in a corner there stood an old-fashioned wash-boiler enclosed in whitewashed brick.

'I don't think I like this game,' Molly said. 'Can't we go and play somewhere else?'

'No, we can't,' Keith said. 'I need a witness. Brace yourself and come inside.' They stepped carefully into the dimness and dust. Molly looked cautiously around to be sure that no corpses were on view. 'Try this on for size,' Keith said. 'The police arrive while John Galloway is out intercepting my car and knocking the driver and then me on our respective heads. They find the place deserted. While they wait, they look in the outbuildings, but there's nothing. So, brandishing their search-warrants aloft like holy emblems, they "effect an entry" as the report will probably say. Now, is there a back drive?'

Molly nodded. 'It comes up on the other side of the woods, starting from around where you got bonked. Sir Peter brought me that way yesterday.'

'Which is when you saw the tin trunk? Right. Now, John G. made off with the body from our car.'

'I don't see what he'd want it for,' Molly said plaintively, 'any more than I want it.'

'Never mind that just now. He must have been getting frantic. He knew that the police were hot on his heels, and because of the delay he was likely to miss his plane. He could be stopped at any time. He might just be able to bluff or bribe his way out, but not with a body in the car with him. And his Land Rover's open at the back, I seem to remember. But he's already had the money for the guns. So he dumps the guns; mainly in the ditch, but two of them fetch up at the roadside where small boys find them. Now he's got the tin trunk to put the body in. He sneaks home by the back drive, and nearly does walk into the welcoming arms of the police; but they're in the house and aren't aware of his return until he's dumped the body and walks in through the kitchen and gets grabbed. He's not going to say anything about a corpse in the wash-house, is he?'

'Not a lot,' said Molly. 'Can we go now?'

'Not yet. So the police finish searching the house, but they don't go back through the outbuildings again. They whisk him away to Edinburgh, leaving Noddy here. What do you think?'

Molly shrugged, 'It's possible, I suppose. But this place is empty. Where's the body now?'

'In the wash-boiler,' said Keith. 'Where else?'

'A good question,' said a fluting voice from the yard.

The emaciated light dimmed further as two men in turn filled the open door.

'And a very probable hypothesis.'

'I could be wrong,' Keith said.

'We shall see.' The speaker was as high and thin as his voice, a lean man with curly hair brushing around a bald crown. His face was mottled and knobbly, but the assembled knobs fitted together into a face that was not measurably different from other faces and yet suggested the kind of callous evil that Keith found the most chilling thing in the world, simply because it was the only thing against which he could not bring himself to react with equal ruthlessness. Molly recognised it too, for he felt her move closer to him. The man was carrying an expensive model of large-calibre automatic, made longer by the fitted

64

silencer. It was a professional's weapon and a good one. The eternal businessman inside Keith thought that, if he could get his hands on that gun, it would pay the shop's rent for a fortnight as well as saving the immediate situation.

The second man was almost as tall as the first but he was broad in a way that reminded Keith of a pedigree bull, and his broken nose and cropped hair only added to the resemblance. Yet he moved with a lightness and coordination that would have suited a man half his weight.

Keith thought that these were almost certainly the 'couple of toughs' who had hired one of Mr Ledbetter's cars.

'Just be good,' said the articulate member of the pair, 'and maybe nobody will get hurt very much. My little friend here will keep an eye on you while I check on your reasoning. And if you're right, I just may do you a big favour in return.' He walked, almost danced, to the washboiler and raised the wooden lid. 'Bingo!' he said cheerfully.

'Leave the body alone,' Keith said. 'It's mine.' He took a step forward and the large, silent man put a hand against his chest.

'Oh no, it isn't! It did belong to Noddy, but it's mine now.' The taller man opened his loose mackintosh and dropped the pistol into a special pocket sewn to the inside. He stooped to reach down into the wash-boiler.

Keith's temper began to go. Common sense would have suggested that the odds were stacked against him. But Keith had hated the taller man on sight; and to have his objective so nearly in his hands and then to see it snatched away would have tried the temper of a far more placid man than Keith. This might be his last chance. If he could lay out the big man he could jump on the other before the gun could be pulled again.

Keith swung at the big man's stomach. In his youth Keith had boxed and had ranked high among amateurs. In later and wilder days he had become a general-purpose fighter of some renown. The blow came from the soles of his feet, gathering momentum from every muscle on the way, and it was aimed at a point below and six inches beyond the parting of the big man's ribs. It was a mighty blow, perfectly timed and perfectly executed, designed to cripple; and the jolt came back up Keith's arm like the kick of a big-game rifle as his fist met a solid cushion of bunched muscle.

The big man blinked. 'Not very friendly,' he said in a deep, husky voice that was hardly more than a whisper. He put out a long arm, took hold of the front of Keith's clothing and twisted. Keith felt as if his chest was being clamped in a vice. He tried to kick. The big man slipped the kick easily and sighed; and Keith, who was no mean weight himself, found himself lifted effortlessly and one-handed, dumped sitting into one of the deep sinks, and pressed down until he was well wedged in. The position was helpless and humiliating, and was made worse by the water from a tap which had somehow been turned on as Keith was pushed against it.

Keith seethed.

The big man pointed with a finger like another man's thumb, first at Molly and then at the other sink. 'Hop up,' he said.

Molly hesitated and Keith heaved impotently in the chilling embrace of his sink.

'If you get out of there,' the big man said in his husky undertone, 'I'll put you back in so hard they'll never get you out.' He put his finger, very gently, on Molly's shoulder. 'Look, I don't like to hurt nobody. It's just all I do well, so it's what I have to do. Make it easy on both of us. Hop up before I have to pick you up and pop you in.'

Molly backed up to the sink and hopped.

'And turn this bloody tap off,' Keith said.

'Leave it.' The taller man had turned to watch the scene. He was smiling and the pistol was back in his hand. 'Leave it running. Maybe it'll dampen his ardour a bit. Now, I'll lug the guts into the neighbour room. No, on second thoughts I'm rather more ruthless than my friend here and he's better adapted for fetching and carrying. I shall watch you while my friend takes poor Noddy out to the car, and if you do anything that I don't like I'll make holes in you where they hurt. Friend, put the body in the boot of the car.'

Keith was in a state of fury; at himself for being caught out, at the thin man for his mocking sneer, at Molly for bringing him out unarmed, and most of all at the icy water which, because the sink's waste was blocked, was rising steadily around his hips. He controlled himself. Molly looked ready to faint. He pulled her head down on his shoulder.

Without visible effort, nor any emotion showing on his battered face, the big man plucked the small corpse out of the boiler. To Keith's dismay, but not to his surprise, the body had been stripped bare and had stiffened into a curled, foetus-like position. As the big man carried the naked corpse the two bore a macabre resemblance to a scaled-up father and child on bath night, and Keith turned his eyes away. He felt sick. Death demanded more dignity than that.

'Now,' said the thinner man, 'I'm going to do you that favour.'

'Favour?'

'Yes. And don't kid yourself, it's a big favour. I'm going to let you live. It's against my instincts, but you've done what I told you so far. You've led us to the body. And if my pure-hearted friend with the strength of ten doesn't bear you any malice for breaking your knuckles on his abdominal wall, then I don't see why I should. But I won't be so complacent next time.' The fluting voice managed to convey a horrid sincerity. 'Now, go home and hide your heads under the blankets. You have a nice little wife,' he told Keith. 'Get in my way again and I might just blot you out and take over.'

This speech had been punctuated by the sounds of a bootlid, a car door and then a car's exhaust as it was backed round to the mouth of the yard. Now came the sound of feet as the big man came back. 'Better we leave now, boss,' he said hoarsely. 'There's folk coming.'

The other man nodded. 'Shall we take the girl along as a hostage?' He was thinking aloud rather than asking a question.

'That's a bad scene, boss.'

'Come on, then.' He backed out of the door, locked it and pocketed the key. Their footsteps echoed in the confined yard and then they were gone in a roar of exhaust and a rattle of gravel.

Through the glass, dimly, a youngish couple could be seen hesitating at the mouth of the yard.

SIX

Inside Keith an enormous fury had been boiling up, and now it exploded into a frenzy of temper that should have burst every blood-vessel in his body. Molly pulled herself out of her sink and dropped to the floor but when Keith, red-faced from emotion and effort, kicked his legs to escape he found himself tightly held both by the sink and by his clothing which had caught on the still-running tap.

There is a word which you must only say when your parachute fails to open. Keith used it six times in quick succession, and several others beside.

Then, 'Scream,' he told Molly.

Molly's first-thought was that Keith resented having only one voice to raise in anger, but then she saw that he meant it. She trusted her husband. She screamed.

With a surge of convulsive energy that would have budged a battleship or turned a road-roller on its side, Keith hurled himself up and forward. Something gave. He was purple in the face, but free. He landed on his hands and knees and scrambled to the door. Behind him, tidy-minded Molly turned off the tap and sighed. Her role was always to follow behind Keith and to pick up after him.

Keith turned the handle and heaved, praying that the lock might somehow have failed to catch. The handle came away in his hand. He hurled it at the furthest window and missed.

The young man had come half-way down the yard.

'Follow those crooks,' Keith roared. 'Try to see where they go.'

'I'll do it,' said a girl's voice, and the blonde half of the couple turned away. Seconds later, a car darted across the end of the yard.

The man came closer. 'Can I help?' he asked.

'They've locked us in,' Keith said. 'Try and break the door down.'

'I'll see what I can do.' The young man set to work with a will, but he was hampered by the fact that the upper half of the door was glazed so that the style was too narrow to take his shoulder. His kicks at the lock shook the whole building, but the door held. Keith drew his knife from its sheath and tried it as a lever, but the blade broke. The handle went the same way as the door-knob. Keith had forged that knife himself, and it had been his companion, worn in a sheath taped across the back of his belt, for many years. In the cold air Keith's breath was steaming, but Molly said afterwards that she half believed it to be smoke and flames.

Keith might well have breathed flames. Added to his other problems was a new and maddening distraction. When he had torn himself free of the sink, he had done so by breaking the buckle of his belt. Now his wet-heavy trousers were determined to obey the pull of gravity, and Keith was determined that they would not. It was the risk of wasting precious time that concerned him, not of cutting a comic figure; but the need to accomplish everything one-handed drove him frantic. Gripping his waist-band with one hand he stumbled to the wash-boiler, grabbed the heavy wooden lid and came back to the door.

'Stand back!'

Straddling his legs to sustain the heavy cloth, Keith swung the heavy lid two-handed and smashed it through the upper part of the door, taking the glass and glazing bars with it. Almost in the same movement he dived through the hole. He intended to somersault and roll to his feet again but his clothing snagged, his timing failed and he came down face first, skinning his palms and his nose. And when he got to his feet his trousers were a soggy entanglement around his ankles.

Keith's fury came to its climax. He would have kicked away his trousers, thrown them away for ever and faced the world without, but they were tapered at the ankles and his shoes were heavy and well-laced. He could envisage the further humiliation. The power of speech left him, and he hissed with rage.

Then a great calm returned at last to Keith, and with it the power to think clearly again. With a jerk that nearly pulled his feet off the ground, Keith raised the offending garment. A piece of cord lay beside the tin trunk, and he tied it around his waist and felt fit to challenge the world.

'Wait for me,' Molly was wailing.

'Stick your head through.'

Molly's head came cautiously through the hole. Keith took her by the scruff of the neck, put his other hand under her middle and lifted her straight through the hole.

'The car,' he said. 'Quick!'

'You're bleeding,' Molly said.

'Never mind that. Come on!'

They cantered round the house. As he ran, Keith dragged the car's keys out of a wet pocket. The young man followed at their heels, shooting out incoherent questions and receiving answers to match. Molly vaulted straight over the side of the car, raising a squeak from the spaniel dozing on the floor; but Keith stood and looked down the valley.

'Two cars,' he said. 'Both going like hell towards Newton

Lauder. About a third of a mile apart. White following red. Was yours the white one?'

The young man said 'Yes.'

'You saw the body?'

'Yes.'

'Right!' Keith dropped into the driver's seat and started the engine.

'Hold on,' said the other man. 'I'm coming with you.' He vaulted up onto the tail and sat himself down, his feet between the seats.

Once again, it was quicker to accept than to argue. Keith took off with a burst of wheelspin that dug grooves in the gravel, but failed to unseat his extra passenger. They hammered over the rippled surface, down towards the old road.

Keith's mind had returned to its usual logical habit, and he was weighing the relative merits of turning left to the police-car near the junction in order to get a radio message to the other car at the far end, or hastening to the police-station, whence the message might be slightly later but more authoritative.

But it would have been against nature to turn away from the direction of pursuit. Keith turned right. The small car, with the hill in its favour this time, gobbled the distance into Newton Lauder. The exhaust sounded a high trumpet-note. The passing countryside blurred and heaved. Keith slowed marginally at the speed-limit signs, had fists shaken at him, and entered the square with a slither and a squeal of tyres. He pulled up outside the police building.

'Look!' Molly pointed. Eighty yards away, at the far end of the square, there was a white car and the fair-haired girl just getting up from it.

'I'm going in,' Keith said quickly. 'You go and find out

what she knows and then join me. And let me do the talking.'

'Don't I always?'

'Frankly, no. Hardly ever. Almost never. In fact, *quite* never.'

'Lying pig!'

With this exchange of endearments, they parted. Molly skittered away across the square with the young man faint but pursuing. Keith loped up the two shallow steps and into the police-station.

The constable standing at the counter to his right was unknown to Keith, but to his relief he saw a familiar figure at the desk beyond. The beefy, red-faced Sergeant Ritchie was an old and well-liked acquaintance, and Keith spoke directly to him. 'I must see the senior officer on duty. Is it Munro?'

'That's just who it is,' said Ritchie.

If the constable had not been listening, Keith would have damned his luck. 'I'll give him the details,' he said. 'Meantime, do you still have cars out at the two places where the old road joins the new?'

'Aye,' said Ritchie. 'Until tonight.'

'And they're still looking in out-going vehicles?'

'That they are.'

'Ledbetter's hire-car, the red Cortina! We've just seen two men drive it off with the body that my wife made a report about the night before last. I think you should tell your men to stop it on sight and hold it, body or no, and follow if that, or any other vehicle, refuses to stop. But tell them to be canny. The thinner man's armed, and the other's as strong as an elephant.'

Ritchie nodded, first to Keith and then to the constable.

73

'Tell the chief inspector that Mr Calder's on the way in to him,' he said, and turned away to the radio.

Keith strode down the short hall, knocked on the end door and entered.

His story was hardly begun when Molly arrived, flushed and breathless. The blonde girl had lost sight of the other car when a tractor had balked her as she neared the outskirts of the town. She had driven on through, to where road-works and a set of traffic-lights were causing a temporary but major hold-up. She was sure that the men could not have passed that point.

An hour later, Keith and Molly were touring the streets of Newton Lauder, Molly at the wheel so that Keith was free to use his eyes. Apart from one halt at the shop for Keith to grab a pair of binoculars, they wove to and fro, street by street, with stops and starts, for another hour or more before Keith directed their path up to a high road above even the hospital. They parked where they could look down on the town.

'That's that,' Keith said. 'I was hoping to spot them before they could get the car out of sight. They didn't have time to make arrangements for somebody's lock-up, and they're not in a public garage. They've probably gone up a side-road and taken to the tracks through the forestry. You could lose an army of tanks in there.'

'You're shivering,' Molly said. 'Your teeth are chattering. And you were supposed to be taking it easy.'

'All in good time.' Keith scanned slowly with the binoculars. 'That bugger Munro didn't believe a word we said. He thinks we're up to something.'

'Well,' Molly said, 'you have been known to get up to things, and you have told him rather a lot of tarradiddles over the years. He didn't disbelieve us altogether. He's keeping the cars out near the junctions for another day or two, and that's quite a response for a small place like this.'

Keith snorted. 'It may be a small place, but the H.Q. here covers an enormous area. They've got plenty of cars at their disposal. And they've collected enough poached salmon and unlicensed guns to make it worthwhile.'

'They won't collect any more,' Molly pointed out. 'They're only stopping the out-going cars, and everybody in the town knows about them by now. There's a red car in Church Street. Keith, why did you say that no doubt they were trying to get the body away so as to cover up the evidence of a murder? You don't really believe that?'

'Don't make me laugh while I'm trying to hold the glasses steady. I think it's the minister's old Viva.'

'What do you think then?' Molly asked plaintively.

'I'll tell you when I have to, Chatterbox.'

On principle Molly made a face, but she refrained from argument. To herself she had to admit that there was something in the impeachment. She went back to the earlier subject. 'The honeymoon couple will bear you out,' she said. 'Their name's Irvine, and they're staying at the Royal.'

'Ah. Well, maybe they will and maybe they won't. Their car was gone by the first time we went through the square.'

Molly made a silent whistle. 'Keith, you don't think those two were fakes?'

'They turned up very conveniently at Briesland House.'

'She said that they'd been interested in buying it. I – er – I said that we'd already bought it.'

'Yes, I expect you did.' Keith put the binoculars down. 'But how many bridegrooms would let their bride go off following a pair of crooks like that? If either of them was going to go, it would have been the man.'

'If he saw you with your trousers down, or heard what you *said*, he wouldn't have left her within a mile of you.'

75

'I don't think it was that,' Keith said. 'You think what you like. But they came to Newton Lauder at the same time as the other two, near enough, just after the body became a body and went missing. And it was the white car that you thought was following us this morning. Did they ask many questions when you spoke to them in the square?'

'None at all.'

'I take it that they were the honeymoon couple that you said were in the shop yesterday? Were they any chattier in the shop?'

'Well, yes,' Molly admitted. 'They did seem to want all the local gossip.'

'And this afternoon all their curiosity had evaporated. That clinches it. Could you see a body being dumped in a car, and find two people locked in a shed, and be asked to give chase, and so on and so forth, without asking a million and a half questions?'

'I suppose not.'

'Suppose?' Keith said scornfully. 'You, my girl, can't even see somebody scratch without wanting to know why it itches and where it itches and when it itches and what it feels like when it does. And by Christ it's getting cold and we're not doing any good here. There's dozens of side-roads and hundreds of tracks and fire-breaks in the plantations and they could be in any one of them. I need dry breeks. And I'm supposed to be taking it easy. Let's away home and *think*!'

While Keith showered and found himself dry clothes and a new belt, Molly dealt with a small group of customers who had been waiting, or making periodic visits. By the time Keith came down from the flat, bringing with him

76

his large transistor radio, they had the shop to themselves.

'Did he have a cold bum then?' was Molly's greeting.

'He did, but he's all right now,' said Keith with dignity.

'Do you really think the honeymooners are in league with the other two?'

'No, I think they're not. Now, keep an eye on the square and shout if you see any one of them or either of the cars. And hush a minute while I think.'

Keith paced slowly to the far end of the shop, paused and turned.

'Control to Panda Three,' said the radio.

'Ignore it,' Keith said. 'I'm only interested in inward messages.' He paced slowly back again, paused and stared vacantly at a rubber decoy duck on a shelf. Panda Three was told to proceed to Willow Brae and investigate the reported theft of a bicycle. Keith came to life again. He snapped his fingers. 'Right. I know what I'd do, in their shoes. And we need help.'

'The police?' said Molly.

'No. It's no skin off our nose who's guilty of what crime. But there's a reward going begging. If we bring in the police, can you see Munro playing fair with me? He could let all his aunts and cousins in on it. We need Sir Peter. I'll watch the square. You give Peter a ring and ask him to come down and join us.'

'You're better on the phone than I am,' Molly said.

'But he can resist me.'

'We haven't had any lunch yet.'

'Never mind that just now. Get on the phone.' Keith looked out at the square, but for all that he saw there he might as well have been blind. By the time the call was finished he had thought the matter through.

'He'll be down shortly,' Molly reported. 'Keith, you're not going to get us into something dangerous are you?'

'We're only looking for information,' Keith said slowly. 'I think that the next thing I'd like to know is who those men were.'

'And how do you propose to find that out?'

'In my experience, there's almost nothing that can't be found out in three phone-calls.'

Molly snorted with laughter. 'Rubbish! If you can find out who those men were in three calls – '

'We'll buy that car, right?' Keith was grinning.

Molly lit up. 'And if you can't we'll forget it?'

'Three out-going calls? You're on.' Keith pulled out the phone-book. 'If Gilchrist thinks he owes me a favour, we may as well cash it in. I'll try the Fettes Avenue Head-quarters in Edinburgh first. That's where Andy Gulliver said he was this morning.'

Keith phoned Edinburgh. Superintendent Gilchrist had left to return to his own office. He would be back in Glasgow by now.

'One down,' said Molly.

'The first call only tells you where your contact is. Second call, he tells you who you ought to be speaking to. Third call, you find out. Got it!' He put down the Glasgow directory and dialled, and the call caught Super-intendent Gilchrist just as he was about to leave for home. The sharp accent came clearly over the phone, and Keith could picture his trim, military-style figure sitting neatly at his desk.

'I thought I might hear from you,' Gilchrist said.

'What did you put Andrew Gulliver onto me for?'

'You know by now, or you wouldn't be calling me.' Gilchrist sounded amused.

'Aye,' Keith said, 'I thought it would be that. But what's going on in Glasgow that makes you suspect a spin-off over here?'

'I was just putting two and two together and making a wild guess,' Gilchrist admitted. 'I spoke to Gulliver on impulse. Was I wrong?'

'No,' Keith said, 'you weren't wrong. In connection with the same thing, we have some hard men around here. Would you be able to identify them from a description? Or could you put me onto somebody?'

There was a pause and Keith could hear Gilchrist, at the other end, tapping his fingers on the desk. Even the rhythm sounded precise and military. 'I'm a bit out of date on that sort of thing,' the superintendent said at last. 'The man you want's Inspector Cathcart. Hold on and I'll give you his number.'

Molly was resting her temple against Keith's and straining to hear the far end of the conversation. 'Only one to go,' she whispered.

'Will he still be in his office?' Keith asked quickly.

'You might still catch him.'

'Do me another favour,' Keith asked. 'He might not want to open up for a strange voice on the telephone. Give him a ring, now or when he comes in in the morning. Ask him to call me, reverse charges, and help me out.'

'All right. I'll do that. Stay by the phone, he often works late. And keep me posted. Cheerio.'

'That was cheating,' Molly said as Keith hung up.

'Not at all. I didn't say I wouldn't have any incoming calls.'

'Can we afford another car?'

'If we syndicate it with the bank manager and the inspector of taxes.'

'And it won't spoil our chance of getting Briesland House?'

Keith gave her a quick kiss on the tip of her nose. 'Baby, if we pull this off we can buy Briesland House and carpet

79

it with the best. And if we don't we couldn't afford to take on anything like that for a few years yet. Now, you pop upstairs and get us a snack.'

There was a last flurry of business as customers arrived on the way home from work. Keith sold a book and a pair of binoculars, accepted a shotgun for overhaul and booked a coaching session for a fortnight ahead. For the rest of the time he stared thoughtfully out of the window.

Molly came back, with soup and sandwiches and coffee all on a tray, just as the phone rang. The shop was empty and normal closing time was near. At a signal from Keith, Molly locked the door.

The voice at the other end of the line was official and disapproving. It had the half-Belfast twang that under-lies the true Glasgow tongue. 'Superintendent Gilchrist said to call you.' The tone suggested that such a command from any lesser personage, such as the Almighty, would properly have been ignored.

'He said that you could help me if anybody could.' Keith paused, but Inspector Cathcart refused the bait. 'We've got some tough eggs with Glasgow accents operating around here.'

'Describe them,' the voice said shortly. Keith thought that he would be dark and sharp-faced, and small for a policeman.

'One of them's a tall, thin, evil-looking bastard, bushy brown hair bald in the middle, brown eyes. His accent sounded like the better end of Glasgow, maybe Bearsden or Whitecraigs; and it wasn't put on, because he used quotations from Shakespeare and Tennyson. He's armed. The other one's about the size and shape of a haystack, very strong but well coordinated, maybe an ex-wrestler. His hair's cropped close, but it looked fair like his eyebrows. Hoarse, whispery voice from somewhere in the Glasgow slums. They go around as a pair.'

'Have you reported this to your local force?'

'Yes. They don't seem very interested.'

'Well, they should,' Cathcart said in a flat and disinterested monotone. 'There's no mistaking those two. The big man's Hughie Spence, and he was a wrestler once right enough. Could have made the big-time but for one thing. If you have to go up against him, and my advice would be against it, go for his head. Nothing else will hurt him at all. But that's why he had to give up the ring, the others all knew that a smash to the head would finish him. He'd be harmless enough but that he's loyal to the other man, and strong enough to break a man in half without meaning it. He'd be sorry after.

'The other's name's Curran. Known as Archie, though as far as we know that's not the name his mother gave him. He came from Bearsden originally, but they tell me he's living in Rothesay now. He's vicious, but no' a lot of guts. If things get tough he'll leave the most of it to Hughie; but he carries a shooter and doesn't mind using it.'

Keith swallowed a mouthful of soup in a hurry, and felt it burn all the way down. 'Can he shoot straight with it?' he asked.

'He didn't used to. He did three years out of a seven stretch, when he might've got clean away if he could have hit the side of a house. Out of nine rounds fired he only hit a pub sign, and that was a ricochet. Anything over ten feet and you're fairly safe. Unless he gets lucky, of course. Or unless he's been taking lessons.'

'Well, thank *you*,' Keith said with feeling.

'Oh. That the lot, then?'

'Hold on, hold on. Who are they working for?'

'Last I heard, they were both working for Frank Hutch. Heard of him?'

'I've heard of him,' Keith said.

'Any more?' Cathcart sounded bored.

'Two. One's more difficult because I only have somebody else's description.' Keith pieced together the fragments of description of the man in hospital, together with the features of the actor said by the hospital porter to resemble him.

'Too vague,' said Cathcart. 'Could be one of dozens.'

'I met another one today,' Keith said. 'About five-ten, fifteen stone, straight brown hair, blue eyes. He looks about twenty-five, but I think he's more. Smooth-faced and chubby. Faint London accent. Sticking-out ears and expressionless eyes.'

'A flashy dresser?'

'Possibly,' Keith said. 'He didn't look very flashy today, but I think he was dressing a part.'

'Sounds like a lad called Wallace. He made London too hot to hold him a few months ago and showed his face around here instead. He was talking to people who don't talk to us. I don't know who he took up with in the end.'

'There's a blonde girl with him. Does that convey anything?'

'Only envy.'

Keith's mind was racing around the permutations. 'Could he have been hired by Danny Bruce?'

Cathcart was silent for a moment. 'Could be,' he said. 'Nothing positive, but I heard that he'd been seen with one or two of Bruce's cronies.'

'I know Bruce as a dealer,' Keith said, 'but can you tell me anything about his operations outside the law?'

Again Cathcart hesitated. 'In confidence?'

'Absolutely.'

'I can't tell you as much as I'd like to. He lives among the nobs of Rutherglen. He's got two perfectly legitimate shops, but you'll know about them. We've known for years that he acts as a fence in a very big way – maybe even the biggest in Britain – but he's quite the most canny man in the trade. He's not above setting up a little rough stuff, but he's got a tough nut of a daughter who makes most of the contacts for him. He never ever deals from his home or from either of his legitimate businesses. He uses *postes restantes*, safe deposit boxes, left luggage rooms for any hot goods, and he meets his clients in an ever-changing series of hotel-rooms, offices you can rent by the day, flats, bed-sits, you name it. He usually has about ten phones, all unlisted. When he goes to some other city to do a deal the goods must travel by post to himself under another name, because he never carries them. And he's the hardest man to follow that I know. If anyone else seems to be going the same way, Danny Bruce turns round and goes home again.'

'Well, many thanks,' Keith said after a moment's thought. 'You've been a big help and I appreciate it.'

'Tell Superintendent Gilchrist. Or, if you want to return a favour, hand me Danny Bruce on a plate. Or, better still, Archie Curran. I'd like to get that bastard before he kills again.' The connection was broken, leaving Keith with a hot ear and a mind awhirl with new data.

'Never try to make a policeman or a second-hand-car-salesman like you,' Keith said. 'Somebody told me that once. I forget who. But he was right. You know, his last comment was interesting.'

'Who's Frank Hutch?' asked Molly.

'So Curran's killed already. I wonder what Gilchrist said to Cathcart to make him so forthcoming. Frank Hutch?'

'Yes, who is he?'

'You must know who Frank Hutch is.'

'Maybe I must, but I don't.'

'He's been in the papers almost every time there's been a big trial in the last few years, in Glasgow anyway. He's about the biggest gang boss outside of London. Branches in Liverpool, Belfast, Dundee and all over. He seems to have been getting more than his fair share of the action. Graft. Corruption. Robberies. Hijacks.'

'Oh,' Molly said thoughtfully. 'I don't know that we want to know him a lot. Or even a little. Is that what you expected?'

'More or less, yes.' Keith came down out of the clouds. 'You had more than your fair share of the sandwiches while I was on the phone, didn't you? How did you manage that and still not miss a word?'

'It's a knack,' Molly said. 'I'll make some more.'

'These'll do, with the coffee. I'm going round the town again. You cash up, keep an ear to the radio and when Peter gets here take him up to the flat.'

SEVEN

Sir Peter Hay had a singular fondness for Molly, placing her somewhere between a favourite grand-daughter and a girl-friend. He spared himself the need to decide between patting her bottom and buying her sweets by doing both and Molly, who to Keith's disapproval had a fondness both for Sir Peter and for sweets, bore with him gladly.

The baronet was a taller man than Keith, but he seemed to be all bones and tangled grey hair. He was a Scot through and through, but his schooling and upbringing had left him ineradicably tainted with the accent of the English landed gentry which he offset by wearing at all times one or other of his many kilts, varying only the modesty or splendour of his accoutrements to suit the occasion. He was the laird of most of the lands for a long way around but, despite his resemblance – cultivated, Keith thought – to a leisured archetype, he deserved the title 'working man' better, perhaps, than many who claim it. He was a notoriously hard-working director on the boards of several enterprises, but the revenue that he earned thereby was ploughed straight back into improvements on the estate, to the joy of his tenants and the despair of his bank-manager. He vacillated eternally on the brink of financial disaster, despite the prospect of dying a very rich man to the benefit of the national exchequer.

It was already dusk when Keith returned, and lamps and firelight cheered the living-room of the flat and made the thought of ever deserting it into a remote dream. Sir Peter's Land Rover was outside the door, and his lanky form was sprawled in the best arm-chair. Molly had made more sandwiches and Sir Peter was chewing on one while, with the other hand, he nursed a glass of the very special whisky that Keith obtained from time to time from an Excise officer at a West Highland distillery who still owed him for a shotgun. When Keith came in Sir Peter raised the glass in salute and enquired after his broken head.

'My head's as almost all right as it ever was or will be,' Keith said.

'Just as long as it's still screwed on the right way. Why the panic message? Your lady wife wouldn't say.'

'His lady wife doesn't *know*,' said Molly.

'She soon will, now,' Keith said. 'Peter, is your Land Rover secure?' He helped himself to a drink and another sandwich while listening with one ear to Sir Peter's assurance and with the other to the muttering of the radio as Panda Four was sent away towards Newcastle to intercept a small van which had driven off from the scene of an accident. When both had finished he asked Sir Peter if, among his directorships, he had any connection with the group of insurance companies represented by Andrew Gulliver.

Sir Peter shook his head. 'Sorry,' he said. 'I can't help you.'

'Yes you can. I wanted to be sure, first of all, that you wouldn't find yourself with a conflict of interests. Now have another dram and listen, in the strictest confidence, to my tale.'

So Sir Peter had another dram and listened, his protuberant eyes opening ever wider and his eyebrows climbing up his forehead. As he spoke, Keith strode about the room, crackling with nervous energy; but Sir Peter sat very still and only moved to stare at Keith when the story seemed to be accompanied by unnecessary or irrelevant detail.

When Keith had finished, Sir Peter stirred and took a small sip from his drink. 'I still don't know what you want me for,' he said. 'Never was much good at puzzles, and this seems to be about as Gordian a knot as anyone was ever asked to unloose.'

Keith laughed and threw himself down on the sofa beside Molly. He knew the baronet of old, and knew that he had caught his interest. 'Don't sell yourself short to me,' he said. 'You're not as dim as you make out, you just like people to underrate you so that you can take wicked capitalistic advantage of them. Anyway, it's not so much brainpower as manpower and useful connections that I want.'

'Explain. I've sat and admired in the past, and no doubt shall do so again.'

'As I said to Molly just now, it's no skin off my nose who committed what crime. If there wasn't a reward going begging, I'd leave it to the police to sort out. But Molly's set her heart on Briesland House, so I want a good whack of the reward so that I can buy the place from you.'

'So far, you ring true.'

'Thank you. Today, I think I just about had my hands on the reward and it was snatched away again. If I go to the police, I'm dependent on getting a fair deal from them. And the officer in charge, at least until I can prove that there really has been a killing, is Munro, who has me breathalysed twice a week in the hope that I'll slip up. I can still get to the reward, but now I have to share it in order to get to it at all. Shall I spell it out?'

'Please do.'

Keith smiled lopsidedly. 'I might never have got the connection,' he admitted, 'except that, between us, Andrew Gulliver and I had said all the magic words in the course of a few hours, and then I got to wondering what Superintendent Gilchrist might know that would make him suggest to Gulliver that he spoke to me. And I have a habit, from years in a business in which you count the other fellow's teeth in case he's a shark, of putting myself in the other shark's place and thinking, "If I had that problem, what would I do?" It's a small step from there to thinking, "If that's what he's doing, what was his problem?" You follow me?'

'Oh yes,' said Sir Peter.

'Putting the pieces together the other way round, what do we have? Andrew Gulliver reminds us that a parcel of gems was pinched not long ago. And here we've got a man who has been accumulating illicit money. He feels the need to get out of the country in a hurry, taking as much as possible of it with him. If he was looking around for a readily portable form of assets, immediately available and at least as valuable abroad as it is here, wouldn't those gems be his most likely bet?'

'That,' said Sir Peter, 'seems logical. But have you any proof?'

'Proof comes later. Next, a man tries to speak to me in Glasgow. He acts as runner and odd-job-man for a dealer who is also a fence in a big way of business. No need to speculate for the moment just what he wanted me to do – that becomes obvious later. Just remember that I'm a dealer and John Galloway was a collector. Then the same man turns up around here, dead. Significant?'

'Potentially.'

'Let's look at it from John Galloway's viewpoint. He knew that a visit from the police must be imminent. For all he knew he was being watched. He would have wanted to buy the gems as quickly as possible and get the hell out. He certainly wouldn't want to trail across to Glasgow and visit with a dealer of dubious reputation; that would certainly have accelerated the activity of the police. Equally, the ultra-cautious Danny Bruce wouldn't want to be within a mile of him. So they would probably arrange for the gems to come across here by the hand of a relatively expendable courier.'

'Noddy Chalmers!' said Molly.

'Exactly. And whatever you may think about speaking ill of the dead, Noddy was not the person you'd hand a parcel of jewels to deliver. He'd've been round to some of his mates in two jumps, looking to substitute inferior stones for the good ones and to pocket the difference.

'So what have we got so far? We've got a theft of jewels in the west of Scotland, a big-time embezzler looking for easily portable goodies, a Glasgow fence making overtures to me and being turned away, and then his runner turning up here dead at just about the time that the embezzler gets his head in a sling with the police. The runner's been shot and the wound looks like a close-range shotgun job. Wouldn't you say that it looked like all of a piece?'

Molly and Sir Peter nodded in unison.

'To round it off,' Keith said, 'as soon as the runner's defunct, suddenly everybody seems very interested in his body.'

'Including you,' said Molly.

'And including two employees of a noted Glasgow gang-leader, and a second group who may represent the fence. So why has Noddy's corpse become so much in demand?'

'Do tell,' said Molly.

'All right. Assume that I'm right so far. Danny Bruce wants to send his parcel of gems through here by the hand of a lieutenant that he trusts about as far as he could spit. He's sending it to a noted collector of antique guns. What might he use as a discreet container?'

89

'Powder horn?' suggested Molly. 'Patch-box?'

'I'd got about that far,' Keith said, 'when I remembered what I'd been saying to Inspector Munro the night before. I hope to hell Munro's forgotten it. Peter, you remember the time I came up to your ancestral dump at Dawnapool, to overhaul and value the guns. How many of the muzzle-loaders did we find were still loaded?'

'Three was it?'

'Four, I think. I forget now.'

Sir Peter sat up straight. 'I've got it,' he said. 'I'm with you now.'

'I'm not,' Molly said, frowning.

'I'll tell you what I think happened,' Keith said. 'Look at it this way. Danny Bruce is selling the gems to John Galloway. He loads them into the barrel of a not-too-valuable antique pistol, by arrangement. Not by arrangement, he chooses a pistol that still happens to contain powder and a ball. He finishes the second loading with a black wad, and sends Noddy Chalmers to deliver it. That way, Noddy thinks that he's delivering a pistol and nothing else.

'Noddy's supposed to meet John Galloway near Briesland House, but not to come to the door in case the house is watched. The ride that runs through the woods would be the most likely place. Molly happens to be out with her camera, not far from the rendez-vous.

'Now let's consider Frank Hutch. Not many crimes are committed around Glasgow without Frank Hutch knowing and taking his cut somewhere along the line. It's quite likely that the gems were originally stolen on behalf of Hutch and sold to Danny Bruce. It would be quite in keeping with what I've heard about Hutch that he should arrange to steal the stones back from Bruce and sell them again to another fence.'

'Ah,' said Molly. 'Now I begin to see.'

'I'm so glad,' Keith said. 'It'd also be in keeping for Hutch to have a spy in Bruce's camp – they say he pays well for information. So let's assume that Hutch was keeping track of the jewels, and when Noddy sets off to deliver them Hutch sends a tough after him to take them away. Quite probably, the tough wasn't told about the stones, he was just told to bring back the pistol.

'The tough catches up with Noddy in Bellcross Woods and tries to take the pistol away from him. They have a struggle. The pistol would be the only weapon to hand for Noddy. He wouldn't know that it was loaded, but it would make a good club – as I have reason to know. In the struggle, the pistol goes off and Noddy is peppered with diamonds and whatever, plus one lead ball. I saw the wound when Big Hughie was carrying the body out of the wash-house, and it's quite consistent with that explanation.

'So the tough has Noddy's corpse on his hands. He decides to remove it, either to hide the evidence or because he did know about the jewels. For some reason that we don't know yet, he decides to pinch our car to move the body in. Perhaps he was using a car that was registered to himself or to Frank Hutch, and if there was going to be blood or corpses found around the place he'd rather that they were found in our car than his. He leaves our car for a minute, perhaps while he hides his own car, and when he comes back Molly's driving off in our car complete with the late Mr Chalmers.

'He gets his car out in a hurry and follows. When he gets to the square, there's the car outside our shop with Noddy still in place. He would have had time to phone his boss for orders, which may have been the first time that he finds out about Noddy's new value. He's told to get hold of the corpse at all costs. So he drives our car away again.

'But John Galloway had been hurrying to the meeting-place. He hears the shot, as Molly did, and sees enough to know or guess what's going on. His Land Rover's nearby, since he was intending to shoot straight off and catch his plane. He probably thinks that he's quitted Briesland House for the last time.

'Galloway knows or guesses that his entire portable assets are now . . . where they are. He becomes desperate. He follows the follower, sees him pinch our car for the second time and shoves it off the road. Frank Hutch's boy is still hanging onto the pistol, intending to get rid of it as evidence, and he tries to bat Galloway with it. But he's still shaken from the crash and Galloway gets the pistol away from him and cracks him on the head with it and lugs him into the trees. I go and turn up and he whacks me on the head too and chucks the pistol into the ditch. Then he dumps all my other guns into the ditch or onto the roadside near where his Land Rover came to rest, so that he can use the tin trunk as a coffin – just in case he meets up with the police but can still bluff it out.'

Molly put her hand up like a child in class. 'But,' she said, 'but you *expected* the body to be in the wash-boiler. How was that?'

Keith looked at her for a second before he answered. 'It's not very nice,' he said. 'Are you sure you want to hear it?'

'I think so.'

'Well, I want to hear it,' said Sir Peter. 'Our little friend can put her fingers in her ears if she wants to.'

Molly snorted inelegantly.

'I wondered what I'd do myself to recover the gems,'

Keith said. 'You couldn't just pull them out with a pair of tweezers.'

'Why not?' asked Sir Peter.

Molly put her hand up again. 'They'd be all over the place,' she said. 'You remember, Keith, that roebuck that you brought in last year. It bolted right onto somebody, and he shot it with a shotgun at about six inches. You skinned it and I butchered and cooked it. Some of the shot was in one clump, but the rest was scattered all through it.'

'I suppose that's right,' Sir Peter said. 'So what would you do? Acid bath?'

Keith shook his head. 'No time to go shopping for acid, and for a bath that the acid wouldn't eat straight through. I think I'd put him into the wash-boiler, bring to the boil and simmer gently for a few hours – all night if necessary. Make soup of him, in fact.'

It was Sir Peter who looked unwell. Molly was only intrigued. 'You mean, like game soup?' she said. 'All the pellets end up in the bottom of the pan.'

'Just that. Run off the soup down the drain, bury the bones, wash out the sludge and you've got your gems back. Not a very pleasant job, but it's what I'd do if it would make the difference between affluence and poverty in foreign parts. He could catch his plane a day later. And the ironic thing is that he just might have got away with it if he hadn't been overcome by compunction and walked into the house to phone and tell the police where I was. And the other man.'

'It may not have been compunction,' Sir Peter said. 'Galloway's a very logical man. He may have realised that if you didn't get attention and one of you died, he could be facing a much more serious charge than embezzlement.'

'True,' said Keith. 'Anyway, next day, two different

couples turn up playing "Who's got the body?" '

Without knowing it, Sir Peter had allowed his other face to appear while he listened. No longer was he the affable, ineffectual aristocrat that Keith knew as a shooting companion and customer. He had become the man of the board-room, alert, thoughtful, decisive and with an authority that money alone never bestows. 'What are the chances of a flintlock still firing after all that time?' he asked.

'It happened this morning in Newton Lauder,' Keith pointed out. 'Given that it's still loaded, remember that most collectors like to see a well-knapped flint in the jaws. If it's been kept in a dry place, the mechanism should still be perfect – with one exception. On lower and medium-quality guns, the half-cock position is nearly always faulty; that's how "Going off at half-cock" came into the language. Oh yes, if the frizzen's down over the flash-pan, it should fire all right.'

'Would there be priming in the flash-pan?'

'If the gun's being carried about, some powder usually shakes through the touch-hole.'

Sir Peter nodded. 'All right,' he said, 'I'll buy it as a working hypothesis, although I think you have a couple of cars missing from the equation somewhere. But your evidence is very circumstantial. You're saying "This is a possible explanation; try to think of a better one". Well, I'm trying, and off the cuff I can't. Perhaps I could have done if I hadn't heard your theory first, but now that I've heard it I must admit that whenever I try to think of another it's your explanation that comes into my mind. But have you any hard evidence? Because, if so, you haven't been very forthcoming to the police about it.'

'I've been honest with the police,' Keith said. 'The fact that they don't believe my story is their fault, not mine. But I don't think I'm obliged to offer them my theories, even if Munro was willing to listen to them.'

'Probably not.'

'They've seen or been told about such evidence as I have. One of them even had his hands on the pistol that I was nutted with, when it was found in the ditch. If he didn't care to examine it, I did. And it wasn't one of John Galloway's pistols. He had several similar pistols with Tower locks, but his were late models with the lock held by two screws. This one was earlier, with three screws. And I took the trouble to look inside the barrel. It had been fired recently, and it had a number of deep scores along the inside of the bore, still bright and shiny. Scratches such as might be made by pellets being fired up the barrel that were as hard as diamond, not as soft as lead.'

There was a two-minute silence; not out of respect for the late Noddy Chalmers, so nearly siphoned down the Briesland House drains, but while Molly and Sir Peter digested and weighed Keith's disclosure. While the silence lasted, Panda Five was sent to relieve Panda Two, and Panda Three reported a chimney on fire in Bloom Street. Keith waited.

Sir Peter drained his glass, set it down and pushed it away. He shook his head to Keith's offer of a refill. 'Very well,' he said. 'Your little Glaswegian friend is now richer than he ever was in his lifetime. What next?'

'Next,' Keith said, 'I'll tell you. Even with that evidence, I don't know that I could convince Munro. If I go to Andrew Gulliver, he'd have to go to the police anyway. Until it's accepted that there's been a murder, Munro remains the officer-in-charge, and he hates my guts. So if

I tell him all about it, and the police later find the body and the gems are recovered, Munro only has to say, "We found the body in the course of our normal enquiries and Mr Calder's information didn't help at all", and I've been slugged on the head, lost two pistols from the collection and been dunked arse-first in freezing water all for nothing. And I've no reason to believe that they have any better chance of recovering the . . . the jewels than we have.'

'They have resources, manpower, radios.'

'They're hide-bound, unarmed and under-manned,' Keith said. 'They might lose it altogether, or miss it for a fortnight, by which time fifty other people might have qualified for a share in the reward. I think I'm on a better bet if I split the chance of the reward with a limited number of people.'

'I don't much like the idea of you going body-hunting,' Molly said, 'especially while that man Curran's running around with a gun.'

'It's time that I asked you something,' Keith said. 'Do you still want Briesland House, or did this morning's stishie put you off it for life?'

'I didn't like what happened this morning,' Molly said. 'But every old house is likely to have something violent in its past. Who knows what mayn't have happened in this flat? I'll be honest, I still want Briesland House more than anything in the world. But only if you'll promise me to be careful.'

'Of course we'll be careful,' Keith said. 'I value my skin and I want to keep it all in one piece.'

'Well, what can we do that the police can't?'

'Two things. We can choose people who can legitimately carry a shotgun around here. That should discourage Curran from waving his pop-gun around. And we can concentrate on the one job instead of being distracted by a thousand problems like the police. Both time and geography are on our side.'

'How do you mean?' Molly and Sir Peter asked together.

'You both know the lie of the land, probably better than I do, but I'll spell it out. The town lies in the bottom of the valley, on the former main road. It was bypassed years ago on the steeper side of the valley, the west. There are still only two junctions to the new road, six miles apart, and those junctions are guarded for the moment. The new main road runs much higher up the hill, and for some reason there isn't just a slope up to it but almost a small cliff.'

'It follows a natural fault for most of the way,' Sir Peter said.

'Whatever the reason, it'd be hard to get up. I could climb it – '

'Damned if I could,' said Sir Peter.

'Well, carrying a body nor could I,' Keith admitted. 'And on the other side, the east, the roads all peter out without going anywhere.'

'I didn't know that,' Molly said.

'I only just noticed it on the map, but it's a fact. We're between the river and the Lammermuirs. A Land Rover might be able to make it, but not a car. People from the farms up that way have to come through Newton Lauder to get out. Peter, that's why I asked if your Land Rover was secure. They may be on the prowl for a Land Rover or a tractor by now.'

'Right,' said Sir Peter with a new enthusiasm. 'Gimme a pencil and paper and we'll assess what's to be done if we're to keep them bottled in.'

'First,' Keith said, 'let's make it difficult for them to get hold of a Land Rover or a tractor. Between us we know all the farmers, foresters and shooting men for miles around. So we put the word around that there's a gang that specialises in supplying them to the black market in underdeveloped countries, believed to be visiting this area during the next few nights.'

'That'll do it,' Sir Peter said, nodding. He made a note. 'At least it'll get them to bring them in from the fields for a change.' He began writing.

'Next, they might think of getting the body up to the main road by using a rope. It's not so easy to put your hands on a long rope when you want it in a hurry. The only shop stocking that sort of thing locally is Ally Sneddon the ironmonger. So I've already called on him. All that he had in stock was two clothes-lines, so I bought them.'

Sir Peter was becoming fretful. 'This is all very dull administrative stuff,' he said. 'Is there not going to be any action?'

Keith looked at him with sympathy. Sir Peter, he knew, had always envied Keith's life, which he believed to be devoted entirely to shooting, poaching and amorous adventures; and Keith had never cared to explain that, whatever grain of truth might have been in that supposition a few years before, he was now a respectable businessman following the paths of rectitude with only minor and occasional lapses. 'There will be action,' he said. 'But first we must get organised. And that means that we must use your contacts. You know the chief constable, don't you?'

'Knew him since we were boys,' said Sir Peter. 'But there's a limit. I couldn't get him to secure your reward for you.'

'No. But we can take advantage of the resources of the police,' Keith nodded to the alert but silent transistor set, 'just as long as we make sure that what we want to know gets reported over it. So phone your boyhood chum. Be the local laird, very concerned about the doings in the town. One of the ministers has been getting onto you about rumours of a body being treated without due respect, and you want the matter dealt with. Get him to take a personal interest in the case. We want the police to go on guarding the junctions for the next few days and to report immediately by radio if either of the two men, or of the honeymoon couple, goes out by car, and most particularly if they come back with a Land Rover. And if a tractor or a Land Rover, or a horse for that matter, is stolen, the fact is to be broadcast to all cars immediately. Can you do that?'

'That much, yes.'

'And he'll go along with you?'

'I think so. If he doesn't, he'll get no more salmon-fishing from me,' Sir Peter said grimly.

'You couldn't get him to make it a full-scale road-block at each of the road junctions?'

Sir Peter shook his grey head. 'That'd be too much to ask at this stage of the game, with manpower as it is today.'

'I thought that,' Keith said. 'And here's the problem. All they've got at each junction is two men and a panda car. What I'd do if I had the body and wanted to take it out would be to drive out past the watch-dogs at one of the junctions – just plain not stop when some young bobby held his hand up. First I'd send my companion out, to be waiting up the first side-road with another car, a stolen one. Then I'd come through with the hire-car and Noddy in the boot, and by the time there was a chase we'd be in a different car. Then away for Glasgow and a bent pathologist.'

'Or an acid bath,' said Sir Peter.

'Or a wash-boiler,' said Molly. 'Plenty of those in Glasgow.'

'That's the weak point, isn't it?' said Sir Peter.

'If the police won't provide road-blocks,' Keith said, 'we must be ready to supply our own, at least until we see how it shakes out. When we looked down from the hill this afternoon, I could see both police-cars. Each of them's placed about half a mile short of the junction. We want a Land Rover and trailer waiting right at each junction, and a load in each trailer to make it too heavy to crash past. Each Land Rover has a transistor set tuned to the police calls, and the driver also watches the head-lights by night and keeps the binoculars on the road in daylight. If a car sweeps through without stopping he pulls the Land Rover and trailer across the junction, locks it up tight and retires into the nearest cover with a rifle or shotgun. That should hold things up until the police get there.'

'Suppose it *is* the police,' Molly said. 'Suppose it's another panda car in an emergency and it goes straight through. It's going to find the road blocked.'

'We'd know it was coming from the radio messages,' Keith said. 'I'll go and see Jake Paterson about more radios as soon as we're through here. Could we borrow your Land Rover, Peter?'

'Use both of them.'

'Both?'

'I bought John Galloway's off him just before he was arrested. I wanted a second one for using about the place and on big shooting days. He was supposed to bring it up to the Hall, although I don't suppose he ever intended to do so. Anyway, the police collected it along with him. When I showed them the documents, they let me take it away. It's up at the Hall now.'

'That's fine. Thanks,' Keith said.

'Personnel?' asked Sir Peter.

'Could you spare Ronnie Fiddler and Hamish Thomson?'

Sir Peter pondered. 'I think so,' he said. 'Your brother-in-law's finished with the roe-deer for now, and I don't need him up north for another week or two. And we'll be buying in day-old pheasant chicks this year, so Hamish doesn't have laying-pens and incubators to deal with.'

'They'll need to be relieved, for sleep and food and so on.'

'There's myself,' said Sir Peter.

'And one more,' Keith said, 'or you'll be averaging sixteen hours a day, which is too much. And I can't help. Somebody has to be free to look for Noddy. What about Derek Weatherby?'

'I doubt it. Farmers are still planting, and there are young lambs to be cared for. I doubt if we could call on any of the farmers. Leave it with me. I'll think of someone.'

'That's fine,' Keith said with real satisfaction. 'You do the briefing. Warm clothes, plenty of fuel and a gun each. Reliefs to take a run along the main road now and again, to be sure that there's no activity there.'

'Right,' said Sir Peter.

'About shares . . .' Keith said.

Molly squirmed in her chair. 'Are you sure we're not too late already?'

'Bless you, not on your life,' Keith said. 'It'll take them time to find that they can't just drive out. They'll have to get a map. They'll do a recce. They'll stop and think. They may want to phone for outside help or instructions, but I've made it as difficult as I can for them. The phone-boxes are all vandalised. The pubs and cafés have coin-box phones, but everybody can hear every word you say. And they can't go back to their hotel.'

'Keith,' Molly said sternly, 'how do you know the public phones are all vandalised?'

'Let's not go into that just now.'

Sir Peter looked disapproving, but Molly was frankly horrified. 'Suppose somebody needs a doctor in the middle of the night,' she said.

'God's sake. The doctors all live in the middle of the town. It's as quick to walk there as it is to phone. So,' said Keith, 'I think time's on our side.'

But Keith was wrong. Noddy Chalmers had already begun his journey out of Newton Lauder.

They discussed the division of any reward, and Keith found that Sir Peter as a negotiator was a different man from the easy-going customer and benevolent landlord that he was used to. In vain Keith pleaded that all the inspiration and spade-work had been his, that Sir Peter would be getting an extra slice of the cake through the selling of Briesland House and that the other two were being paid anyway; when the bargain was closed Keith found that he and Molly were to share forty per cent of the reward between them, Sir Peter would take another twenty and the other helpers ten each. If pressed, Keith would have to admit that the division was fair; but he would have preferred fairness to be tempered rather more in his own favour.

'What do I do?' Molly asked nervously.

'Not a lot,' Keith said, 'and none of it rough. To-morrow's Saturday, so the shop'll have to stay open. You look after the shop, listen to the radio and act as a centre of communications. And you'll have to take turns with me at listening to the radio through the night.'

'I will, will I?' Molly said gloomily. 'I don't know that

I'm so sold on Briesland House after all. What are you going to be doing tomorrow?'

'Ah,' Keith said. 'I think I'll give Andrew Gulliver a ring and see if he'd like to come pigeon-shooting.'

'You'll *what*?'

'I can kill three . . . four . . . five birds with one load of shot,' Keith explained. 'First, I've got to fill Gerry Reynolds' waterers for him anyway. Two, I can look over the town from a high place, spy out the land and watch for movement. Three, I can think. Four, I can ask Andrew some very particular questions.'

'And five?' Molly asked.

'Five, I might even bring back a few pigeons for the pot.'

EIGHT

For most of his life, Keith had been preoccupied with activities governed by such variables as dawn and dusk, moonrise and the tides and, until his recent marriage, by the comings and especially the goings of husbands and families. When you adopt poaching as a vocation, and extend your activities over the whole spectrum from the common rabbit to the human female, you learn to manage with little and irregular sleep. Keith had become a master at sleeping when sleep was offered and remaining awake when the offering was of a different kind. He needed his gift that night.

What with the detailed briefing of the patrols, constant competition with Sir Peter for the use of the telephone, several hours of contingency planning, a lightning visit to a neighbouring shopkeeper and a final tour of the town it was late before Keith got to his bed. Jake Paterson, the shopkeeper, was prevailed upon to reopen his shop for the sale of three radios which could receive the police wave-band, at a price which, even after the discount which Keith negotiated, added fervency to Keith's yearning for the reward money.

Even when bedded, Keith lay for an hour before it was time to waken Molly for her turn at monitoring the radio and the telephone. As soon as he could be sure that Molly was fully awake, Keith let himself slide away into oblivion. It seemed only seconds later that he was being shaken by the shoulder.

'Time?'

'Three. Keith, I think it's important. They just told one

of the cars to investigate a report of somebody pinching clothes-lines out of back-gardens in Rowan Close.'

'You're right, it is important.' Already Keith was wide awake and hurrying into his clothes. 'Damn it all to hell, I've guessed wrong. But somehow you don't expect a couple of big-time hoodlums to go around pinching clothes-ropes. Hold the fort. I'll make a cup of tea when I get back.'

'Be careful you *do* get back,' Molly said. 'I don't want to live in Briesland House on my own.'

'You'll have to, if you go on at me,' Keith said. 'I'm always careful.'

A bagged shotgun and a powerful hand-lamp were ready beside the door, and Keith grabbed them and ran. Despite a thick sweater and a quilted anorak the cold bit deep into him as soon as he was outside. The moon was high, outshining the street-lamps, and everything sparkled under a white rime of frost. Keith had to struggle to free the door-lock on the little car, struggle again to lift the bonnet and replace the rotor-arm and to scrape a hole in the frost on the windscreen with his fingernails. He ducked into the car. It felt claustrophobic under the fabric hood. The shotgun and lamp went down by the passenger's seat. The engine started at the second try. Three blips of the throttle and Keith set off with a slither on the icy road. A black rectangle showed where another car had been standing further down the square.

Peering through his peep-hole, Keith turned south. It was a slightly longer way, but it would pay off when he reached the main road. The road still offered some grip and he was able to keep up speed. Gradually his peep-hole in the windscreen enlarged as the car's heater began to overcome the bitter chill.

Keith knew roughly where the panda car was lurking.

Even so, it appeared round a curve before he was expecting it and he slid to a stop almost under the hand of the shivering constable. Keith jumped out of the car and ran to open the boot. The constable glanced inside. Under that moon he had no need of a lamp. The trees were white against a jet-black sky.

'Going a bittie fast, weren't you?'

'Hurrying a wee bit, but well inside the legal limit,' Keith said. Deep inside himself he was saying a prayer. It was hours since he had had a drink and his blood-alcohol would pass a laboratory test; but the breathalyser is less discriminating, and if the officer cared to produce his little plastic bag Keith's breath might well turn the crystals. 'I doubt I'll be in as much hurry coming back,' he added.

'You'll not? Why would that be, Mr Calder?'

'Not unless the husband's come home again. Well, I'm getting in out of the cold.' He ducked back into the car.

'I just bet you are,' said the constable in a different voice. He waved the car on. Almost for the first time, Keith blessed his reputation.

Half a mile and two bends on, where the Land Rover would have been waiting at the junction with the main road, there was only a motor-scooter at the roadside and a small figure with a shotgun under one arm and a radio under the other. Keith skidded to a halt.

'You heard?' he asked.

'The clothes-line message? Ronnie heard it, so when I came to relieve him just now he went up.'

'Hop in,' Keith said.

The little car was a tight fit by the time another person, another gun and the radio were fitted in. Keith spurted away uphill on the main road. 'I didn't know Sir Peter had picked you for fourth man,' Keith said. 'Will your father manage without you?'

'Dad knew the frost was coming,' said Janet Weatherby. 'He said there'd be little to do except the lambs for a few days. All the same, he didn't want to come away himself. So he sent me.'

'This may not be work for a young girl.'

'I've as much need of a share in the reward,' Janet pointed out. 'Maybe I have to spend my life as the daughter or the wife of a small farmer, and maybe I don't, but I've a better chance of breaking out of it, or of having some fun to look back on, if I've had a wee bit money of my own. I could get a car like this, and all the latest gear.'

Keith sighed and felt old. 'Maybe greed will make up for experience,' he said. He roared up the deserted road, holding hard to the wrong side so that he was looking down on the countryside below. The lights of Newton Lauder were ahead and to his right. Like the constable, he had no need of his lamp. The barrier rails partly obscured his view, but he was reasonably sure that he was not passing any human activity. Then he saw the Land Rover and trailer stopped up ahead and his brother-in-law beside it, waving. He pulled up and climbed out.

Ronnie's big figure came towards the car. 'One down there,' Ronnie said gruffly. 'The other drove off towards Edinburgh when he saw this.' He hefted the rifle in his hands.

Keith could see a car higher up the road. Below, a lanky figure was running carefully down the track, away from Gerry Reynolds' cottage. The roof was just below them.

The rifle in Ronnie's hands looked like the Voere three-o-eight that Ronnie kept for the red deer. 'You'd wake the whole town with that,' Keith said. 'Brought anything quieter?'

Ronnie leaned back into the Land Rover and brought out his silenced small-bore.

'Put the fear of God into him,' Keith said. 'But don't hit him this time. Not much, anyway.'

'Right,' said Ronnie. He raised the rifle.

'Then stand guard here 'til we come back. Back in the car, Janet.'

They set off again, tyres shrilling for the first instant on tarmac thawed by the heat of the car. Even on the uphill gradient the little car came up to speed in a few seconds. Keith drove with all lights out, using his lightest touch on the wheel. The road showed up well under that moon. They flashed past the other junction, and Keith saw what seemed to be a tiny face peering out at them but knew that it was Hamish Thomson, his face reduced to a small circle by the luxuriance of his hair and whiskers.

The other car had a start of a mile, but in a few minutes Keith was coming up on it fast. He recognised it as the small Renault belonging to a neighbour and usually parked in the square. Hughie Spence's huge shoulders seemed to fill the space between the back window and the windscreen. The Renault was slowing.

'He thinks he's got away,' Keith said. 'He's looking for somewhere to turn.'

'He's not far off the junction for that road that goes away towards the Moorfoot Hills,' Janet said.

'Good idea. Let's chase him up there.' Keith switched on his lights.

As if the twin beams had physically thrust the other car forward the Renault bolted away. Keith let it gain a little distance. Then a sign showed up and a junction, and the car in front turned off to the left.

'Ha!' said Keith.

'How are you going to stop him?' Janet asked.

'I don't know that I have to,' Keith said. 'Harry never leaves more than a sniff of petrol in his tank. He was siphoned once, and thinks it's going to happen every night. My tank's full. Is your gun loaded?'

'No. You taught me to make sure I was unloaded when I got into a car?'

'Right. But now's different. Unbag my gun for me and then load up.'

Keith followed, fifteen yards behind the other car. Big Hughie Spence was no more than an ordinary driver; a better one could have tried a thousand tricks to ditch or lose the car behind, but the big man only tried to pour on speed and run away. The sports car, built to go fast and to hold the road, clung tight without effort.

'I mind you're a left-hand shot,' Keith said.

'Yes.'

'If he doesn't stop before, we'll stop him at the loneliest place for miles around. It's a few miles on yet. Be ready, and when I give the word fire a warning shot. Think you could knock one of his wing-mirrors off?'

'I think so, if you hold the car steady.'

'Just remember all I taught you, and aim a bit high. I don't mind buying Harry a new mirror, but not a whole damned wing. He may stop before then. If he looks at his fuel gauge he may realise that he has to get us off his tail, maybe stop us and snatch the key or disable the car. He's strong enough to tear off a couple of wheels, is that bugger.'

'Really?'

'Yes, really. Well, just about. I promised Molly we'd be careful, so this is what we'll do. When he stops I'll take the car clear and we'll both pile out with guns and cover him. He'll probably see sense. If he tries a rush, fire one warning shot and then, if he keeps coming, blast him.'

'But I can't just – '

'Oh yes you can just,' Keith said forcibly. 'Remember, this is for real. You came on a treasure-hunt, you brought a gun, you must have accepted that there was a chance that you'd have to use it. If he's coming towards you, and you have reasonable cause to believe that he means to attack you, then you've every right to shoot. Just remember that we were on a fox-shoot, so we had guns with us, and then we saw Harry's car being stolen. And be careful that he doesn't turn away just at the moment you pull the trigger – if you get him in the back we'll have a lot of explaining to do. Have you got that?'

'I ... I think so,' Janet said.

Janet's presence was a nuisance and a potential embarrassment.

Keith could hardly have failed to know that he was attractive to women; they had told him so too often, in deeds if not in words. Vaguely he supposed that this was due to his combination of gipsyish good looks and brass neck. It amused him, sometimes, to make a complimentary and mildly suggestive remark to a woman; be she nonagenarian or nun, she would look at him and glow. For any woman could see, although Keith never did, that he was predisposed to love each and every woman. He understood and responded to their bright, gentle minds. He liked the pitch of their voices and listened to what they said. He adored their preoccupation with feminine things. And he loved, whenever he could, their smaller, softer, rounder bodies. Keith, without knowing it or even being consciously polite, announced his lovingness in every tone of voice, every hint of body-language, and it came as a fresh and pleasant surprise to him each time that a woman responded to his unconscious emanations of reverence and lust.

But Janet, now, was a problem. For years she had had a schoolgirl crush on him that expressed itself in a teasing manner and a tendency to be there whenever he turned around suddenly. While she had been too young for it to be taken seriously, her crush had not mattered. But Janet lived too near his own doorstep, and now that she was in her later teens it mattered like hell.

Keith decided that, no matter what the night might bring, he would keep his hands to himself.

The car in front slowed and then held steady at thirty.

'He's seen his gauge,' Keith said. 'He's thinking it over. Be ready.'

Janet rearranged the guns, to free her feet.

Suddenly brake-lights shone out and the Renault slewed and stopped diagonally across the road. Keith braked straight and almost ran into its back corner. He slammed the sports-car into reverse. Janet was already out of the car. Keith spurted back ten yards, and as he did so he saw the big man erupt from the Renault like a charging rhinoceros. Keith jerked the hand-brake on, grabbed his gun and opened his door while the car was still sliding.

He was too late. As he straightened up, the big man, light as a dancer, darted forward. Keith heard the twin, high barks of Janet's twenty-bore. The muzzle-flashes were bright in the moonlight, and Keith knew that she had shot high. Then Spence swept her up into his arms. Her empty gun clattered in the road.

Keith cursed silently. The bloody girl had chickened

out at the last instant. She could have blown the big man's brains out, with certainty and impunity.

Keith lifted the gun. 'Don't hurt the girl,' he said quickly, knowing the man's strength.

In the light of his own headlamps he saw the man grin over her shoulder. 'I'll not hurt the wee hen. Just the reverse.' The hoarse whisper was pitched up over the sound of two engines running. 'Now drop the shooter or I'll squeeze her 'til her guts drop out.' He tightened his grip and Janet's breath came out with a whoosh, drifting away on the frosty air like an isolated smoke-signal for help. Her feet pedalled frantically in the air.

In spite of Janet's plight, Keith could almost have laughed. The big man was quite unaware how tight and accurate a pattern a shotgun would throw at such short range, and in sheltering behind the small girl he was like an elephant hiding from a rifle-bullet behind a lamp-post. 'You're showing eighteen inches of leg under her feet,' Keith said. 'Which foot do you want me to blow off?'

Hughie Spence lowered the girl until her feet were on the ground and ducked behind her. Janet drew breath again and closed her open mouth.

'I can see the top of your head,' Keith said.

'The lassie – '

' – might be deaf for a day or two, but you'd be in a lonely grave by the roadside.' Keith took two paces to the side. 'Now I could blow your arse right off,' he added.

The big man's answer was to release his pent-up strength in hurling the girl straight at Keith. It was what Keith would have done in the circumstances, so it came as no surprise. He stepped aside and let her go by to fall against the car. His side-step took him also out of the way of Big Hughie's follow-up rush, and as the man checked Keith reversed his grip on the gun and swung it like a club. The big man caught it behind the ear. He half-turned, dropped to his knees and leaned tiredly against Keith. Past the cropped head, Keith found himself looking into Janet's face, but in the harsh contrasts of the car's lights he could not guess how fit she might be for more action.

'Help,' Keith said. 'Get him off me.'

Janet's voice was shriller than usual. 'What's he doing to you?'

'He's kneeling on my foot, and I think he's breaking it.'

Between them they toppled the big man, and watched him lie groaning in the road. Keith lowered the muzzle of his gun. 'I was bloody lucky this didn't go off,' he said. 'It'd have cut me in half. I'll cover the bastard this time, and I shan't be so soft. Take a look in the Renault's boot.'

Janet sniffed. 'I notice that you didn't shoot him either,' she said.

'And I don't remember seeing you club him with the stock.'

Janet was still going to get the last word. 'At your prices, I can't afford to damage my gun,' she said, and turned away. In a few seconds he heard her voice again. 'Nothing in the boot but some old clothes-line. What was I supposed to find?'

'Er . . .' For the first time, it occurred to Keith that if Noddy Chalmers' naked corpse had, in fact, been in the Renault's boot then he, Keith, might have had two inert bodies to cope with in addition to the now stirring Hughie Spence. He thought that a man couldn't be expected to think of everything. 'If it's not there,' he said, 'don't bother. Turn the two cars around.'

By the time that Janet had turned the two cars, backing carefully round in the narrow road, and returned to stand beside Keith, Hughie Spence was sitting up, shaking his head groggily and fondling the lump behind his ear.

'Take the Renault,' Keith told Janet. 'Drive slowly. I'll
be right behind. We're making for the junction where you
left your scooter. If you run out of juice I'll tow you, but
freewheel as far as you can.'

The big man got to his feet and stood, swaying wildly
and shivering. 'You're not going to leave me here?' In
his state of alarm, his voice became almost normal. 'I'll
freeze to death.'

'Listen, Squire,' Keith said, 'you can freeze to death if
you want to. It wouldn't bother me one damn bit. Keep
moving and you'll be all right. You can be sick if you
want,' he added. 'You'll feel better.' It was the voice of
experience.

The big man was made of sterner stuff. He shook his
head and nearly fell over. 'I should be in hospital,' he
said.

'You should be in a zoo. Tell me where the body is and
I'll take you to hospital.'

Spence snorted. 'I don't know where the body is. I
didn't put it away.'

'Archie Curran did that, did he?'

Spence stared at Keith. 'You know that, do you?'

'Yes. And so do the police.'

'If you know that much, you can maybe find wee Noddy
for yourself.'

'I'll maybe do that,' Keith said. He thought that Spence
was lying, that he knew perfectly well where the body was,
and if Keith had had his brother-in-law along they might
have been able to beat the information out of him. But
with only the girl for help . . . 'Start walking,' Keith said,
'or if you can't walk, crawl. Dawn will be up soon. You
won't die as long as you keep moving . . . *that* way.' Keith
pointed west. 'After I've seen the lassie home I'll come

back, and if you're *this* side,' he pointed back towards Newton Lauder, 'of *that* line,' he drew a line with his heel across the road in the frost, '*then* you die. Got it?'

Hughie Spence looked as if he were going to nod, but he thought better of it. 'I got it.' He hesitated.

'When you meet Archie Curran,' Keith said, 'he'll know that we haven't heeded his warning. So what do you think would be the sensible thing for me to do now?'

'I told you I got it.' Spence turned carefully, and lumbered away westward.

Janet was still standing close to Keith. 'What did he mean?' she asked. 'You said not to hurt me, and he said, "Just the opposite" or "Quite the reverse" or something. Did he mean – ?'

'Yes,' Keith said, 'he did. He says he doesn't like hurting people.'

'Would he really – ?'

'Probably.'

Janet rubbed herself against him and laughed, a high giggle with a tremor in it. 'You were in a hell of a hurry to spoil our fun weren't you?' she said. Keith decided that she was joking. He could feel shivers running through her. He realised suddenly, with the intuition that he had about women, that she was in a state of high sexual excitement, and he wondered if she had really been joking. He wondered if she even knew it herself.

Keith tried to disperse his hormones by thinking of something more interesting. After a few moments he decided that there was nothing more interesting than being rubbed against by Janet. 'Get in the car and drive,' he said. 'And not a word to the others about the near squeak we've just had. I don't want Molly worrying.'

'I'm not fit to drive yet.'

'You never were and never will be. Drive anyway.'

'Pig!' Obediently, making of the deed a gesture of subservience to the dominant male, she got into the Renault
and started off with a jerk.

Keith took a last look after the big man and saw him
stagger to the roadside and stoop over the heather. Keith
nodded sympathetically. He knew how it felt.

As he followed the Renault's lights, Keith thought that
it was high time that Janet found a husband. Not even in
his wildest days had Keith preyed on the teenage daughters
of his friends. Not until they were safely married. He
wondered if Molly's brother would care to take her on.

The drive back took half an hour. The moon was setting
and they were in full darkness by the time they regained
the main road. Then the lights of Newton Lauder
appeared in the valley. They were already on the downhill run before Janet ran out of petrol. The Renault rolled
decorously on at barely more than walking speed.

Sir Peter's old Daimler was parked window-to-window
with the Land Rover at the northern junction, and Keith
saw the two anxious faces watching. He stopped and
opened his nearside door. 'Ronnie's waiting just above
Reynolds' cottage,' he said. 'Join us there.' He slammed
the door and accelerated away, overtook Janet, stopped
behind the other Land Rover and was in time to stand in
the light of his own lamps and wave Janet down. The
Daimler and the Land Rover with Hamish drew up behind.
Keith became aware that both the trailers were heavily
loaded with dung. They all packed into the Daimler for
warmth.

'You first, Ronnie,' Keith said. He looked at the silhou-
ette of his tough, craggy brother-in-law with affection, but a

corner of his mind was envisaging Ronnie married to Janet but away at the stalking for weeks at a time.

'Aye,' Ronnie said. 'Well. I sent a couple of rounds after him, like you said.'

'Did you hit him?'

'You said not to, so I didn't,' Ronnie said virtuously. 'Damn near, though. I bet he crapped his breeks – he was leaving a vapour-trail behind him going down the track, and then he took one hell of a toss over one of the ruts and skited on his lug for about ten yards. It took him a mintie to get to his knees, and what a target that was! Keith, man, I could have put a round up his bum without touching the sides. But I just bounced one off the track beside him. I heard it ricochet, though, and I thought it might bring the polis up if they was to hear bullets screaming above the roof-tops. So I held my fire.

'He went on down to the bottom like a bolting hare, except that he didn't run in a curve. And at the bottom he stopped and shook his fist at me. And you'd said not to hit him much, you didn't say not to hit him at all, so I took a shot at his fist. I think I was over him, though. A rifle shoots high, shooting downhill, and I didn't allow enough for that, or maybe the bastard went and moved. He didn't hang about after that.'

'I bet,' said Hamish.

'And another half-hour later, the wee wireless reported Mr Ledbetter's hire-car, the red one, going out with a tall, thin, baldy streak of piss driving – they didn't put it just like that – but no sign of any dead bodies in it.'

'That's right,' Hamish said. 'He came out past me, but he'd stopped at the police so I let him go by.'

'That was fine,' Keith said. 'He knew he couldn't get the body out on his own, so he took off.'

'What happened to the other fellow?' Sir Peter asked.

'We chased him into the hills,' Janet said airily.

'He'd stolen Harry Glynn's car,' said Keith. 'He could have had it for all I cared, but Noddy might already have been in the boot before Ronnie got here so we had to chase him up. He stopped on the moors and I belted him with my gun. I think I split the stock.'

'My barrels are dented,' Janet said.

'Never mind,' said Ronnie. 'Keith'll take the dents out for free.'

'I'll think about it,' Keith said.

'So,' said Sir Peter, 'where do we go from here?'

'We've done the first job,' said Keith. He yawned. 'Unless the honeymoon couple have got their hands on Noddy, which seems unlikely when you remember what Spence and Curran were doing, we've boxed the body in and chased the opposition away. I don't suppose they've fixed up a rendez-vous this side of Glasgow. I suggest that we knock off for now. Noddy could be hidden anywhere for miles around, and I'm not dashing around in circles doing a search. We think and watch. But since they were trying to get out this way we'd better take a look through the woods along this side of the town. I'll meet Andrew Gulliver as planned. I suggest that the rest of you grab some food and an hour's sleep and meet up at dawn to walk through the woods looking for disturbed ground, a parked car, any sort of container. Take dogs. And if you meet Gulliver, don't let on what it's all about.'

'I'm on,' said Sir Peter, and there was a general murmur of agreement.

'Janet, are you sure you're fit?' Keith asked.

'Fit for anything.'

'That's it, then. Walk the woods, then have a proper sleep. We'll meet at my place, say six p.m., for a meal, a think and a talk.'

NINE

With a cooked breakfast inside him, Keith took the spaniel down to the square just before dawn. In a few minutes Andrew Gulliver came walking down the square, his bagged gun over his shoulder. 'God, it's cold!' he said. 'You've brought decoys?'

'There's a bag of decoys in the boot,' Keith said. 'I don't think we'll need them, but it costs little to be prepared.'

'Where are we going?'

'You'll see. Can you squeeze in?'

'I can try.'

'Take Tanya at your feet.'

They fitted themselves into the car and moved off. A few yards along the square, opposite the police building, Keith turned off to the left and in the dim light of early dawn they could see the way that ran straight as a ruler, first a road serving small Victorian houses, becoming a lane that began to climb through the woods that ran down the west side of the town, and then a steep and narrow track, barely more than a path, that climbed between overgrown hedges up to Gerry Reynolds' cottage.

Keith stopped the car short of the woods and, walking softly, they separated for a dawn roost-shoot. It was tricky, exciting sport, walking softly through the woods, waiting for the canny pigeon to choose their moment and clatter out on the blind side of the man who, fumbling with frozen fingers, had to take them in snap shots as they crossed a small patch of sky. Each shot put ten other birds out, and by the time dawn was up the tree-tops were empty. The occasional pheasant, knowing well that it was out of season, only scuttled into the bushes at the approach of man.

They met back at the lane. The men were happy, the spaniel ecstatic.

'It's not so cold now,' Keith said.

'Not quite.'

'You take a seat in the sun and watch whether any flight-pattern develops. I'll bring the car up and do my good deed for the day.'

Keith fetched the car and humped out a carrier of warm water. A hundred yards from the lane and on either side of it were two clearings where Gerry had the feed-hoppers and watering-points for his birds. Pheasants were chortling in the bushes as Keith lugged his container to the first clearing. Gerry's water-troughs were old tyres halved around the circumference. Each was fed from a water-drum, but the drums were frozen. It was easy to tip out the ring of ice from each half-tyre and refill it, and, each time, the water was surrounded by pheasants before Keith was out of sight. From the second clearing that Keith visited, a large flock of pigeon got up.

Keith found Andrew Gulliver sitting in a patch of sun by the gate to the track. 'How are the police getting on?' Keith asked with great casualness. 'Has Galloway said anything yet?'

'Not a word. Silentest chap ever.'

'And your own enquiries?'

Gulliver sighed. 'The accountants have been working like the beavers they are; and the police have been both helpful and astute. This isn't for publication, mind you. As near as we can figure it, Galloway's share must have been slightly over half a million. Sounds a lot, doesn't it? But it isn't as much as it used to be. We've tracked some of it to a Swiss bank account, and I suppose the lawyers will have a grand time for the next ten years or so trying to get it back. It looks as if Galloway did a certain amount of speculating with the rest, probably trying to wash it clean, and he's had a few losses. I suppose that part's gone for ever.'

'So how much are you looking for in this country?'

'Something just short of two hundred thousand.'

Keith watched the flight of some distant pigeon. 'And you still don't know where it is?' he asked casually.

'We know where it was, which isn't quite the same thing. He had literally dozens of accounts with banks and building societies, and over the last week or two he seems to have been converting it all into cash.'

'Cash only?' Keith asked. 'No bearer bonds?'

'Cash so far. Tens, twenties and hundreds.'

'Hundreds?'

'I don't suppose he wanted hundred-pound notes, but a hundred-and-eighty thousand pounds is devilish bulky if it's all in smaller notes.'

'How would that amount compare,' Keith asked slowly, 'with the value of the missing jewels, the ones stolen from Prestwick?'

Gulliver looked at him sharply. 'So that's what you're thinking! We've been wondering along the same lines. The stones were insured for two hundred and ten thoussand.'

'Would he pay as much as a hundred and eighty, to a fence?'

'Why not? He was in a seller's market. And he could get full value for them, somewhere far away.' Gulliver stubbed out his cigarette and stood up. 'If you've finished picking my brains, let's do a little of what we came for –

as the girl said to the soldier. They seem determined to come in over there.' Gulliver nodded towards the clearing where Keith had put up the pigeons.

'Probably some spilled grain around the hopper,' Keith said. 'In a frost like this they'll come in anywhere they can still get a meal. I'll tell you what we'll do. I've got to walk up to the top anyway. You go and make yourself a hide over there, where the birds are coming in, and when I've done my boy scout bit up top I'll stay up there for a while and see if they don't follow the line of the hedges each time they're disturbed. Maybe we can keep them on the move between us.' Keith picked up his water-carrier. 'Thank God this is empty!'

'Can't he get a vehicle up to the top?'

'Not up the track. It's too narrow in places, and he won't cut the hedges back because they're the only good partridge cover he's got.'

'There's devotion for you. How does he manage?'

'Most years there's pasture on one side or the other and he can get his Land Rover up that. When it's ploughed both sides, as it is this year, he has to walk until the harvest's cut. So he gets in bulk stores before the last of the ploughing's done, and only has to carry up fresh food. Sometimes he gets heavier stuff let down to him from the main road. He ran out of cartridges at Christmas and I had to throw him down a few hundred, box by box.'

Gulliver laughed. 'It wouldn't suit me,' he said.

'It suits Gerry all right. He spends his time walking anyway.'

Keith, too, was used to walking, but his year or two as a shopkeeper had taken the edge off his fitness and by the time they reached the top he was sweating under his thick clothes and puffing gently. Tanya was panting like an old-fashioned steam-engine. She was also puzzled. In a manner which she had considered little short of masterly, she had homed in by scent on two separate pairs of partridges in the bottom of the hedge, and each time her master had called her off and let the red-brown birds whirr away unshot. What was wrong? It was a shooting day, wasn't it? She let Keith see that he was in disgrace.

Above their heads, early traffic murmured unobtrusively on the main road.

Keith found the key of the cottage and opened the door. Gerry Reynolds had left his electric heating on at a low level; the cottage was cool, but the water was still running. Keith refilled his container, but before he left he went through the place thoroughly. When Keith was finished Gerry might still have some little secrets, but Keith could be quite sure that the cottage contained no hidden corpses and no Glaswegians. He locked up and, after a moment's thought, put the key back under its stone.

The morning sun was flooding down now, but there was no real warmth there. It was as if the sun shone only because the sky was too cold for clouds.

To the north and south of the cottage, gorse-bushes grew along the foot of the cliff, and here two more feeding-places had been established. Again Keith tipped out the rings of ice and refilled the half-tyres for the waiting birds.

Duty done, Keith established himself behind the big water-barrel at the gable-end of the cottage, and set out his gun, cartridges and binoculars on the lid. He was armed with a five-shot repeater, not because he had any particular fondness for that type of gun but because of the possible reappearance of one or more of the enemy. With a double-barrelled gun he could fire one warning shot and then he would have to shoot to kill.

Andrew Gulliver was firing occasional shots below, and

soon a flight of five pigeon came up the line of hedges towards him. Keith took four of them and could have had the fifth but that he had promised himself always to keep one round in the gun. When he was sure that no more were following, he went out and set the four up as decoys and returned to hiding.

There was a lull in the bird movement, and Keith was free to look around. Below him, the town was waking up. At the end of the straight line made by the track, the lane and the road, the doors of the police-station were open with a trickle of early enquirers going in and out. Keith wondered if he should take one of the rings of ice from one of the watering-troughs and bowl it down the track, to see if it would go all the way down and across the square and up the two shallow steps of the police building and along the corridor and right up to Chief Inspector Munro's desk. Maybe it would flatten the smooth-faced Hebridean bastard. On the other hand, maybe it would flatten somebody else. Keith decided not to bother.

Cars were moving, pedestrians and cyclists were heading for work or for play. Tiny to the naked eye, through Keith's binoculars the faces were quite clear; but none of them belonged to the people that he was watching for.

With occasional breaks when Gulliver's gun sent a few birds streaking up towards him, Keith studied the woods around the town. It was too early in the year for the deciduous trees to be clad with leaves, but there were enough conifers in the woods to spoil his view of the ground, and the square miles of forestry were impenetrable to the eye. He could see nothing suspicious. In the fields, the only moving figures were the farmers and the sheep they were tending. Once he spotted Hamish, and then Sir Peter, moving through the nearer woodland.

Keith stamped his feet. The sun was a little warmer

on his face now, but his body and legs were in shadow and the barrel radiated a penetrating chill. He turned the binoculars on Briesland House. The sun was slanting across its face, throwing long shadows from a wisteria that would be bright with flowers later in the year. Yesterday, the garden had seemed all green, except for splashes of white and yellow from daffodils and forsythia and early rock-plants, but now he could see purples of aubretia and early rhododendrons. The place had charm, dignity, serenity, space and, Keith thought cynically, it *looked* expensive. Covetousness came over him in a wave, and it was not only from his desire to give Molly what she had set her heart on. Come what may, he was going to own Briesland House. He tried to check the roof for missing slates, but the distance was too great. A female figure came out of the front door and disappeared around the side.

The pattern of the morning remained the same – occasional flurries of birds and then long periods during which Keith could scan the countryside and the town or, more importantly, could think. One at a time, he put himself in the place of every known participant in the drama. Then he conjured up imaginary characters and tried to fit them into the unproven parts of the story, but the pattern seemed complete without them.

Andrew Gulliver had arrangements for an early lunch and for the rest of the day, so at eleven-thirty Keith sent Tanya to pick up his birds while he stowed his gear in his game-bag. He visited the troughs again and broke the new skins of ice before starting down the hill. The descent was steep and the going tricky, and Keith thought that a stranger trying to run down that track by moonlight would certainly take, as Ronnie had said, 'one hell of a toss'. Archie Curran would be short of some skin. Keith began to feel better about his own face and palms.

Gulliver came out of the wood to meet him. He had a good bag of pigeons. 'But I put three down that I can't find,' he said. 'They may be runners.'

Keith sent Tanya to search among the trees. He thought that he could trust her not to bring him a pedestrian pheasant, but at least he knew that her soft mouth would bring it to him unharmed. The two men sat down on a log. Tanya brought the first bird and was sent in again.

'Are you offering a reward for the missing money?' Keith asked.

Gulliver nodded and looked at him quizzically. 'Ten per cent., the same as for the gems.'

'What if the money's been spent buying the gems?'

Gulliver laughed. 'Nice try, but you can't have it twice. One recovery, one ten per cent. Unless of course you could recover both the jewels and the cash that had been paid over for them. Are you going to try for the cash?'

'Oh, surely,' Keith said. 'I'll just wave my magic wand. How bulky would that parcel of jewels have been?'

'Not very. You could put them all in one pocket.'

'I need to know a bit more accurately than that,' Keith said.

'I could work out an approximation based on value, average size, number of stones and specific gravity, with an allowance for air-spaces. When do you want it?'

'Now?'

Gulliver looked pained, but he got out an envelope and a silver pencil. 'Without any packing material,' he said at last, 'the least volume that you could get them into would be about five cubic inches.'

Keith sat in thoughtful silence. Tanya brought the second bird.

'A couple of your pals went by while we were shooting,' Gulliver said, 'and if I were allowed one guess as to what they were up to, it'd be that they were looking for something in connection with the money or the jewels or both. Possibly that dead body, about whose existence your local chief inspector is expressing scornful incredulity. He's convinced, by the way, that you're setting up a smoke-screen to cover some mischief that you're planning for the future, but I'm not so sure. At a further guess, you had some ploy on last night and it didn't quite come off. And I think I should give you a friendly word of warning. If you have any information that I don't have, you'd better bring it to me or to the police.'

'Can you guarantee me exclusive access to the reward?'

'You know I can't. If somebody else contributes to the recovery . . .'

'Or if ten other people help?'

'That's the luck of the draw. But the longer you hold off revealing your information, the bigger the chance of your being forestalled. What's more, if you have something, and you don't tell the police, and it transpires that a chance to recover either the money or the jewels is thereby lost, you personally will be wide-open to litigation. And if that fails we'll ensure that nobody will ever give you insurance cover for anything again. You understand what I'm saying?'

'I understand,' Keith said.

'So take my advice, and not chances. Right, that's enough on such sordid topics between friends. Thank you for an excellent morning's sport. I'll be staying on for a few days, so would you like those birds?'

'Thank you, I would,' Keith said. 'And in return I'll pass on one juicy morsel of information to you. While I was up at the top, I put the binoculars on Briesland House and I saw a woman come out. At that distance . . . well, it could have been Mrs Galloway. I'll leave you to think that over while I go and see how Tanya's getting on.'

Deep in the wood, Keith suddenly found Tanya beside him with the last pigeon lolling dead in her mouth. She sat and delivered it into his hand. Already pigeon were coming back into the wood, skimming with quick wing-beats over the tree-tops. Keith followed their line and came out in the clearing with the feed-hopper and the water-trough. Pheasants ran into the bushes, a big cock rocketed up through the branches and from beyond the hopper a flock of pigeon exploded upwards.

Keith walked over to the hopper. Grain lay around it on the ground, and more seemed to have been thrown into the nearby bushes.

'Well, well, well,' Keith said to Tanya. 'Precious grain all over the ground, so what would you suppose would be in the hopper?' Tanya gave a quick bark. 'You think so, do you? Grain taken out to make room for it? Well, let's just take a look.'

The hopper was made out of a former oil-drum but had been fitted with a loose lid. Keith's face clouded, and he paused. Then, quickly, he lifted off the lid.

The body was curled up and crammed inside.

Tanya looked at Keith's face and whined.

Keith raised his head to call Andrew Gulliver, but closed his mouth without a sound. Carefully he put the lid back on the hopper and they walked back out of the wood into the cold sunshine.

'Time you opened the shop again,' Keith said. He pushed his plate away and covered his mouth politely. 'How was business, by the bye?'

'Not bad at all,' Molly said. 'I took almost a hundred quid this morning. Why don't *you* open the shop?'

'Too much to do. I'll do the washing-up for you.'

Molly blew a raspberry. 'You only break things,' she said. 'I know you do it on purpose, but we still can't afford it. You go and open the shop and I'll do whatever it was you were going to do.'

Keith grinned at her. 'All right. It'll let me get on with Lord Fowler's gun. You go and search Bellcross Woods.'

'Oh no I won't, thank you very much. I'm not going into those woods alone again until this is all over. And I don't think you should either. It's all very well keeping watch and telling the police as soon as you know something. If you can get the reward, I'm all for it. But I don't want you bumping into that man Curran, not for anything.'

'He'll hardly be back from Glasgow for hours yet, if he comes back at all. And I'll be carrying a gun.' Keith yawned, stretched and got up. 'Do you want sixty-odd woodies for the freezer?'

'Not if I have to pluck and dress them all.'

'I'll leave you a dozen, and drop the rest into the game-dealer on the way by.' Keith kissed her tenderly and pinched her bottom. 'I'll see you later.'

'Not if you leave me a dozen wood-pigeon to pluck, you won't. And I thought you were going to do the dishes.'

'I'll do them when I get back,' Keith said from the other side of the doorway.

Molly sighed and started to do the dishes.

Keith looked back into the kitchen. 'I asked the other four to come for a meal tonight,' he said. 'Six o'clock.'

Molly dropped a plate.

TEN

At six that evening Sir Peter and Janet arrived on the doorstep, with Ronnie and Hamish not far behind. The meal, Molly explained, was far from ready since His Nibs (pointing without any great affection at Keith) had not relieved her in the shop until half an hour before. Keith, who was fighting back a succession of yawns, led them through to the small living-room and gave them seats.

'Keith Calder,' came Molly's voice from the kitchen, 'just what the devil were you doing with my sugar?'

'Pouring it down a gun-barrel,' said Keith. 'What else? Now, who's for a drink?'

Even the dispatch of her brother with a mammoth goblet of sherry failed to pacify Molly. Janet took a gin-and-tonic, the others whisky. The atmosphere was far from festive. After the high hopes of the night before, when each had mentally committed the reward money to projects of delicious extravagance, frustration and irregular sleep had produced a mood in which cheerfulness and optimism were forced.

'A grand drop of stuff, this,' said Sir Peter, looking at the light through his glass.

'It's time more was fetched,' Keith said. 'Ronnie, next time you go north – '

'Glad to,' said Ronnie. 'And may your customs mannie never pay off his gun!'

'It was a very expensive gun,' Keith said. 'He's barely keeping pace with the interest.'

'Amen to that!' said Sir Peter, and the men raised their glasses. Sir Peter gave a quiet cough that called the meeting to order. 'Now that we've slept,' he said, 'it's time to consider where we go from here.'

'Aye.' Ronnie stuck out his formidable jaw. 'If anywhere. Seems to me we've given it a shot and got nowhere.'

'We may not have hit the target yet,' Keith said, 'but we've not missed it either. In fact, we did what I hoped to do. Now, if you lot want to give up and drop out, you can do so with my grateful thanks, and I'll go reward-hunting on my own.'

He was smiling faintly. Ronnie thought that he was bluffing. Sir Peter thought that Keith was onto something. Janet thought that he was very good-looking. Hamish tried to draw attention to his empty glass.

'We gave the woods a good going-over,' Sir Peter said thoughtfully. 'I don't think that we missed much there.'

'I'm afraid that you did,' Keith said. He drank from his glass, yawned and wriggled himself lower in his chair.

There was a quick silence. 'What, then?' asked Sir Peter.

'You missed the little matter of a corpse in one of the feed-hoppers.'

This time the silence was not absolute. Every person present made a tiny noise of surprise or enquiry. The effect was of a distilled question, audible but unverbalised. Sir Peter was left to verbalise it. 'So it's all over, then?'

'It's hardly even begun,' Keith said. 'For a start, it wasn't the body that we were looking for. It was the corpse of the young man, Wallace, the supposed bridegroom.'

Molly came to the kitchen door. 'Oh, that poor girl!' she said. 'On her honeymoon!'

'I wish you'd stop thinking of them as a genuine honeymoon couple,' Keith said patiently. 'Sergeant Murchy says the police haven't seen hide nor hair of either of them since we last saw them in the square. Their luggage, which is two-penn'orth of nothing, is still at the Royal.'

'But if they're both dead . . .'

'We've no reason to believe that they're both dead. Molly, I never saw the girl close to. Was her hair real blonde?'

'It wasn't even real hair, it was one of those nylon wigs.'

'And she could have another dozen wigs of different shapes and colours with her. No wonder I've been wasting my time looking for a blonde,' Keith said. Molly sniffed. 'I know who she might be,' Keith went on. 'Was she a wee bit taller than you with much bigger tits, brown eyes, a squarish sort of face, a big mouth and a small nose coming to a wee knob?'

'That describes her,' Molly said, 'except that I don't think all that bust was genuine either.'

Keith ignored the comment. He knew for a fact that it was genuine. 'That's Danny Bruce's daughter. I wondered why the girl went to follow the other car instead of the man, but she'd not want to stay and be recognised. Her name's Mary. She's reputed to be the tougher of the two, although she was always pleasant enough to me – the few times that we met.'

'She was, was she?' Molly sniffed again, and went back into the kitchen.

'She was very quick on the scene, wasn't she?' said Janet. 'Did she come to keep an eye on Noddy, or how did Danny Bruce know to send her?'

Keith frowned at the ceiling. 'She had time enough. As soon as Noddy failed to report back, they knew something was wrong. Danny sends his little girl through to watch his interests, complete with hired gun. They're dropped off here, and hire Ledbetter's car. They wouldn't know what they were looking for at that stage, but the local gossip would soon have told them what was known about events. The only person involved and still walking around loose was me. And Molly, of course. They follow us. We lead them to the Briesland House. They see the other two making off with Noddy. That should give them the clue they need. The girl follows up and sees where they're headed for. Maybe the other two take the car into the woods until dark, complete with Noddy, or maybe they leave Noddy in the hopper and come back later. Wallace, with or without Mary, lurks in waiting. But he makes a mistake, and the unfortunate Wallace – '

'Who has with Noddy bled,' said Hamish.

'Exactly – ends up in the hopper.'

'That explains Mary's little lamb,' Janet said callously, 'but what about Mary?'

'At this point,' Keith said, 'that's anybody's guess. She may have been off-duty at the time and know nothing. She may have seen it all and stayed out of trouble. She may even have grabbed Noddy for herself.'

'Hardly work for a girl,' Hamish said. ' 'Course, she may be dead too.'

'Mary Bruce is a tough nut,' Keith said. 'I'd back her in a bout with Dracula, so if we come across her don't treat her as a sweet little maid. And I don't think she's dead. I thought I saw Mrs Galloway at the door of Briesland House this morning, but now I'm betting that it was little Mary. She'd need somewhere to lie up, and she knew that it was empty but still furnished. I suspect that she's phoned her father to be ready with a reception party when she gives the nod, to catch Spence and Curran between here and Glasgow. She'd let them get Noddy out of town for her. She couldn't do it on her own – if she still is on her own.'

'There's been no sign of any other strangers around

here yet,' said Sir Peter. 'But the important question is this. Have you reported finding the body?'

'That's the question, isn't it?' Keith agreed. He picked up the whisky-bottle. 'Let me top up your glasses.'

Janet looked shocked, and Molly darted through from the kitchen. 'Keith! You haven't left that poor young man in a pheasant-hopper? It's not decent. You'll have to tell the police at once.'

Keith fought back another yawn. 'I don't suppose he's minding an awful lot,' he said. 'The mannie's dead anyway. He's safe from crows and foxes, and the weather's gey cold. There'll be nothing coming over him while we talk about it.'

'All the same –'

'Something's burning.' That got rid of Molly. 'It's a problem. I'm not very bright just now, but I think I can spell out our options.'

'You'd better do that,' said Sir Peter. He sounded colder than his usual self. 'But I must say that I can't like the idea of leaving the young man's body out there.'

Keith took another swallow and put his glass down. He rubbed his smarting eyes. 'As I see it, we have three choices. Firstly, we can tell Munro that we found the body. It would have one advantage – he could hardly go on disbelieving in the other one. They'd certainly keep their cars at the junctions, and they might even be persuaded to make proper road-blocks. Against that, they'd be searching all over the place. Worse, we wouldn't be able to get out of making full statements to the police – and to the press.'

'Would all that really matter?' Janet asked.

'It would if we still wanted to earn rewards. The second option would be to sit tight and say nothing. But then the panda cars will be withdrawn, and Noddy might go for a ride.'

'And the third option?' asked Sir Peter.

'We make an anonymous phone-call, reporting the body, stating that there's a link with the other one and implicating Archie Curran and Hughie Spence. That way we get the road-blocks, hamper the opposition and keep our freedom of action; but we might lose our claim to that part of the reward if some prying bobby happens on Noddy's corpse.'

There was a babble of discussion, but Sir Peter broke into it. 'You said, "that part of the reward". Is there another part?'

'Oh yes,' Keith said. 'There's another part all right. I think it's time you heard about my day before we come to any conclusions about what we tell the police.'

'You're a cold-blooded brute,' Molly said from the door, 'but life must go on. You'd better come and eat, all of you. Eat plenty, because when that husband of mine gets talking about himself he forgets to stop.'

'I married her for her witty monologues,' Keith said. 'Bring your drinks through with you.'

They settled themselves in the cramped dining-room under the framed copies of sporting prints from an old calendar. Molly served a thick, peppery soup to suit the weather. Keith offered a wine, but the men elected to stay with the whisky.

'Your day,' said Sir Peter.

Keith had been beginning to nod but he dragged himself awake. Between mouthfuls he summarised his two talks with Gulliver. 'I did some thinking while I was up on the hill,' he went on, 'so as soon as I'd had a bite to eat I went out to Bellcross Woods. I visited Briesland House first. I told you I thought I saw Mrs Galloway there, but it may have been Mary Bruce. If it was, she was wearing some of Mrs Galloway's clothes. There was nobody there, but a small pane's been broken beside the front door. You'd better get that fixed, Peter, and I think we should visit the place regularly.

'Then I went and searched the woods. I was following up something that you'd said, Peter. At first I couldn't find a damn thing of any use, but that was when I thought I was looking for a car. But when I'd thought some more while I was tramping around in the woods, I realised that a motor-bike would make more sense.'

' 'M not with you,' Ronnie said with his mouth full

'The man took our car, remember? That seemed a gey queer thing to do. But suppose Noddy had a motor-bike. So the other man came on a bike too, because it'd be tricky following a bike by car. You'd lose it at the first traffic-jam. So I looked again, and I found a motor-bike lying down and covered with dead branches and grass. I gave it a careful searching, but there was nothing worth noticing about it unless you count a Glasgow registration.' Keith's voice was slurring.

Sir Peter paused with his spoon in the air and directed a searching glance at Keith. 'How much sleep have you had, last night and today?' he demanded.

'I tried to get him to go to bed,' Molly said, 'but you know how thrawn he can be when he feels like it.'

'I'm used to going without sleep,' Keith said.

'Not for the last couple of years,' said Sir Peter. 'And I'll tell you something else. In your exhausted state, that whisky'll hit you like a club.'

'Thanks,' Keith said. 'I'll be careful. So then I came back here to relieve Molly at the shop. Oh, and I took the dents out of your barrels, Janet. I won't charge you, because I did a lot more thinking while I was getting on with it.'

'You seem to've been doing a lot of thinking,' Molly said, 'but is it getting us anywhere nearer the reward?'

'I think so. Two motor-bikes arrived at Bellcross Woods. Noddy got shot. The other man put him in our car but Molly drove it away. So what does he do?'

'Follow on the other bike?' Janet suggested.

'Right. Probably he'd take the nearest one to hand, if he wasn't to lose touch with our car. Then he drives away from outside here with the car. So what happened to the motor-bike?'

'Stayed here,' said Hamish.

'No,' said Keith, 'I don't think so. I think I chased him up on it. And when I came round after being nobbled I asked the police to return it to its loving owner, not knowing that same owner was either dead or unconscious at the time.'

Ronnie clattered his spoon into his plate. 'Why are we interested in bloody motor-bikes?' he asked sourly. 'There's been a wheen of thinking going on, but not a damn bit of results.'

Molly might have said much the same thing a minute before, but only over her dead body would anyone else say a word against Keith. 'Don't you dare talk like that,' she told her brother. 'You never had a thought in your life. But when Keith gets thinking, something always happens. And don't *smirk*,' she added. 'I didn't say anything funny.'

'We're interested in motor-bikes,' Keith said, 'because Andrew Gulliver worked out that the gems would take up about five cubic inches, and the most I could think of getting into a loaded Tower pistol was about half as much. And that, by the way, is what I was doing with your sugar,

Molly, before I relieved you in the shop. I tried it out and I'm about right.'

Sir Peter thumped the table and made the dishes jump. 'Sorry,' he said. 'I'm used to a heftier table. Never mind. So it was a *pair* of pistols that Danny Bruce sent through as a container?'

Keith struggled with a yawn that screwed his face into a caricature. 'That's right. Noddy had two pistols with him. He took one out, either to be ready for John Galloway or because he knew he was being followed and it was all that he had to defend himself with. He could use it as a club, or poke it through a pocket and pretend that it was a modern revolver. When it went wrong and he got shot, his attacker didn't know that there should be another pistol, and so didn't look for it.'

'But what's-her-name,' Molly said, 'the girl with the falsies, she'd know that there was a pair. Of pistols, I mean.'

'She would. But she'd be wondering whether we had the other one, or Curran, or the police. If she got around to wondering whether it wasn't still in Noddy's motor-bike, would she know what bike to look for? Do you think she'd recognise a bike belonging to one of her father's irregular employees? She might have had the foresight to note the number down before she came, or to phone her father for it – if Danny Bruce ever knew the number, which wouldn't be certain.'

'Where's the bike now, then?' Janet asked.

'If it's not in the police pound, it's probably still out in the square. There's usually a whole row of them by day, but not by this time. Want to go and have a keek through the front window?'

Janet jumped up and went through to the living-room.

She came back to the doorway. 'There are two out there. There's a big, new-looking one; a Jap, I think.'

'No.'

'And an older one, a bit tatty-looking.'

'That could be it,' said Keith.

'Shall I go and look?'

'Yes, do. Lift the saddle and see if there's anything in the tool-tray. Ronnie, just in case somebody's lurking, would you go with her.'

'Aye. I'll do that.'

'Bolt the door again when you come back.'

'Bolted doors?' said Sir Peter when the two had gone.

'I didn't fancy looking up from my meal and seeing Archie Curran looking at me. Now maybe I can finish my soup.'

'It'll be cold,' said Molly. 'Shall I heat it for you?'

'It's fine, girl, don't fash yourself. Dish up the meat.'

Molly dithered. 'Aren't you going down? Aren't you even going to watch from the window? Don't you want to *know*?'

Keith gave her his soup-plate. 'If they find something, they'll come back and tell us. I've done enough running about. Now I'm going to let everybody else birl around.' He yawned again, enormously. 'Dish up the meat, there's a good girl.'

'Sound philosophy,' Sir Peter said. 'Hamish, with our host's permission you might fetch the bottle through.'

'Aye, Sir Peter.'

'But – ' Molly was almost dancing with curiosity and indecision.

'Either it's there or it's not,' Keith said. 'Going and looking won't make a damn bit of difference.'

'That's right,' said Hamish, coming back with the bottle.

'Hamish – ?'

'I didn't bother looking,' Hamish said. 'Knowing a minute sooner isn't worth a second's precious drinking-time.'

'But I want to seeee!'

'That meat certainly smells good,' said Sir Peter.

His word was law to Molly. She started serving the meat.

'Which hopper is the body in?' Sir Peter asked.

'Bottom of the hill, north of the lane.'

'My patch, I'm afraid.'

'Shame on you!'

'It is indeed. But I have an excuse. Your friend Gulliver was not very far away.'

'You should have thought of an excuse to open the hopper. Something that wouldn't give the game away. "I wonder if young Gerry's got enough grain in his hoppers," you should have said.'

'I should, shouldn't I? Didn't think of it at the time. Tired,' Sir Peter said in explanation.

'I'm tired now,' Keith said. He sounded surprised.

'By George, you must be!'

'Oo, that smells good!' said Janet and they looked up. There was a frozen moment of suspense. Janet and Ronnie stood over the table with carefully blank faces. Then Janet said 'Taraah!' and whipped out a large flintlock pistol from under her coat.

'You bolted the door again?' Keith asked.

'Aye.'

'Oh, get on,' Molly said in anguish. 'Is there anything in it?'

'I meant to remind you not to pull the trigger,' Keith said. 'We might have had diamonds and emeralds patter-ing down on the roofs of Newton Lauder. Or be rendering one of you down in the wash-boiler.'

'I'm no' daft,' Ronnie said. 'First thing I made her do was to flip the frizzen back. But she was scared to look inside, and she'd not let me take a keek.'

Keith sighed and took the pistol from Janet. He pulled the ramrod out of its sleeve and pushed it down the barrel. 'Empty!' There was a groan around the table. Keith used a knife-blade to reflect light down the barrel, and squinted inside. 'No it's not, by God!' he said. 'Not quite. There's a patent breech and something caught in it.' He upended the pistol and rapped the butt sharply with the handle of the carving-knife.

Something tinkled into the saucer beneath and everybody leaned forward. A small stone lay in the saucer, flickering with cold, green fire.

'So somebody did recognise Noddy's bike,' Sir Peter said at last.

'Looks like it,' Keith said. 'We got there too late. Sorry!'

Janet put out her finger and touched the emerald gingerly. 'I didn't really believe any of this,' she said. 'Not even when we met that man up on the moors. It all sounded too story-book to be true. But now it's all coming home to me. Here's a little bit of the real stuff, which we found by our own efforts. It's really happening.'

'It's a start,' Hamish said.

Ronnie grunted. 'Yon yin's all we'll get, though,' he said.

Keith succumbed to a series of enormous yawns. He took a pull at his drink and dragged himself back towards a sort of wakefulness. 'At a guess,' he said, 'after we've paid our expenses so far, your share of the rest of the reward on that stone might come to about a tenner. Do you want to settle for that and drop out?'

Ronnie hesitated. He had seen Keith's inspirations working out before. 'My time was worth more than that,' he said gruffly. 'I'll not drop out while I'm losing. But it fair breaks your heart, losing the chance of half of it like that, for we'll be awful lucky to get so near it again, or the body either.'

'It'll not be far away,' Keith said. 'And it's not a half we just missed. Only a quarter.'

Ronnie was the first to find his voice. 'Here we go again,' he said. 'More nights' sleep up the spout. Sitting all night in a Land Rover, in a frost fit to neuter you, just in case yon big bugger and his poofy friend decide to come back body-snatching.'

'There's a thaw forecast,' said Sir Peter. 'Warm front coming in from the west tomorrow.'

'And now the bad news,' Ronnie said gloomily.

'Wind your neck in, Ronnie,' his sister told him. 'You nearly made over a thousand quid in the last twenty-four hours.'

'Aye. I was going to fly out and see the next World Cup.'

'Well, Keith says there's three times that still to come. So if you're going to gripe, go and gripe somewhere else. But, Keith, can't we all sleep tonight?'

'That's for discussion,' Keith said. 'Tonight I'm certainly going to sleep a sleep that'll make Wallace and Noddy look quite lively.'

'You should be in bed now.'

'I'm all right. I'm used to it.'

'I think you've got unused to it,' Sir Peter said, looking

at him closely. 'But, Keith, if you're still with us, what about tonight?'

'I don't think they'll be back tonight, it's too soon for a fresh plan, but we'd better not take any chances. Could we manage one patrol until dawn? Just a quiet car – your Daimler? – going to and fro and up the lane and back?'

'We could do that,' Sir Peter said, and the others nodded. 'You don't think that we should try to watch up at the top?'

'They wouldn't come the same way again,' Keith said. 'Not so soon. They don't know how we got onto them so quickly last time.'

'But suppose they decide to go out past the police, the way you said first of all?' Molly said.

Keith nodded heavily. 'That's why my advice is an anonymous call about Wallace's body. That way we make it very difficult for them, and at the same time we keep ourselves free to look around, and we give away no information where it might be used to pull the reward out from under us.'

'Take that as agreed,' Sir Peter said after a pause. 'Now explain why you said that what was in the pistol was only a quarter of the whole.'

Keith rubbed his face vigorously, and pulled his eyes open by muscular effort. 'I thought of one more thing. How was John Galloway to pay for the jewels. And I wondered what I'd do if I were him, and then if I were Danny Bruce. They wouldn't want to meet, in case one of them was being watched. Bruce wouldn't send the gems on appro, to an embezzler who's just going to flee the country; and Galloway, when he's just going to have to split in a hurry, isn't going to pay a fence in advance for hot stones. I don't think they'd trust each other enough to deal on a half-in-advance basis, and neither of them would trust Noddy Chalmers with a tenth of that much cash.'

'Post-dated cheque?' Hamish suggested. 'Or a joint account requiring both signatures?'

'That would link them, which neither would want. And Galloway was raising strictly cash. I was hoping to find a clue on the motor-bike.'

'Nothing like that,' Ronnie said.

'It would take up quite a volume,' Keith said thoughtfully. 'Galloway was raising cash in tens, twenties and hundreds. You don't see many hundreds about. You walk into a bank to draw out several thousand pounds in cash and ask for it in hundreds, and I bet they don't have more than a very few. He may have been drawing out around a hundred and sixty thousand quid, which might be around ten thousand bank-notes. Maybe . . .' He held the palms of his hands about eighteen inches apart. 'You don't carry that in your hip pocket.'

'He'd have to send something back by Noddy Chalmers,' Sir Peter said.

Ronnie stirred and cleared his throat. 'Once you start this business of thinking what you'd think if you were the other idjit, it gets quite easy,' he said. The others looked at him. It was his first original thought within their memory. 'I mean,' he went on, 'I ken fine what I'd do if it was me arranging it. I'd have Galloway cut the notes in half and send them through the post. Then when Noddy delivers the jewellery, he brings back the other half. That way of it, nobody gets a chance to swick the other, and Noddy can't make off with anything worth having.'

There was a rustle of interest. 'Mr Galloway would have been taking his half into the woods with him,' said Janet.

'Where's his Land Rover now?' Keith asked.

144

'Up at the hall and quite secure,' Sir Peter said. 'But, Keith, when I got delivery of it I went over it thoroughly with Ledbetter's mechanic. We couldn't have missed a parcel the size of ten thousand half-bank-notes. Was nothing found on him when he was arrested?'

'According to Andrew Gulliver, nothing,' Keith said.

'It could be just corners of notes,' Hamish said suddenly.

'Or even just one number off each note,' Molly said.

'Even part of a number would be enough, wouldn't it?' Janet asked. 'Say the last so many digits. It'd be very small. Like confetti.'

'I'll bet that's it,' Ronnie said. 'That's just the way those two twisting buggers would have it fixed.'

Keith came out of a shallow doze. 'The arrangement would be for Galloway to meet Noddy. The sensible thing would be to take the two pistols into the cab of the Land Rover – one at a time, which would explain why one of them was still on Noddy's bike. While he's supposed to be examining each of them, out of Noddy's sight, he uncorks the barrel, tips out the gems and stuffs the barrel with bits of bank-note and corks it up again. "Return these to Mr Bruce with my compliments," he tells Noddy. "They're not quite what I want but tell him to keep me in mind for next time." And away goes Noddy, none the wiser. But Frank Hutch sends a hard man to grab the jewels and, he hopes, the money. Noddy gets shot. John Galloway gets arrested. The police don't find anything on him, nor on the hard man who fetches up in hospital unconscious.'

'So it must still be in the Land Rover,' Molly said triumphantly.

'Unless he took it back to Briesland House.'

'I'll take a look in the Land Rover,' said Sir Peter.

'Try all round the cab first,' Keith said. 'He'd not want to get out and lift the bonnet in front of Noddy.'

Ronnie was again visited by inspiration. 'Transmission-brake,' he said. 'They have a wee hatch under the middle seat, for getting at the brake. That's where I'd put it.'

They looked at each other in satisfaction. Each was quite convinced that the crucial contribution had been his or her own.

Keith gave way to a yawn that threatened to dislocate his jaw. 'Have a look,' he said thickly. 'Find anything, pop note through door here, get together early tomorrow. Be ready . . . go through for day. Glasgow.' His voice trailed away into a mumble.

'What did he say?' Ronnie asked anxiously.

'I think,' said Molly, 'I *think* he said something about driving some sort of van.'

'That's what I thought too,' Janet said. 'An *ice-cream* van.'

They waited expectantly, but Keith was sound asleep, his chin on his chest but his fist still clenched firmly around his glass.

'Och, rubbish!' Ronnie said. 'It couldn't have been that. If he thinks I'm driving an ice-cream van around Glasgow on a freezing Sabbath, he's dottled. Anyway, the thing just doesn't make sense.'

ELEVEN

Refusing all offers of help, and especially those from Janet, Molly got Keith to his bed where, having had only two hours' sleep in the previous forty, he slept like the dead. The others held a conference. Hamish, who spoke so rarely that his voice was as unknown as his whiskered face was familiar about the town, was elected to make the anonymous phone-call; which he duly did, assuming for the purpose an American accent that would not have deceived an aborigine in Borneo.

And while Keith slept there was much coming and going around Newton Lauder. The police reacted to Hamish's phone-call initially with only qualified belief, but a solitary constable was sent to examine the feed-hopper. In due course a report was radioed in by a constable who found himself alone with a corpse in a dark and icy wood and, his sergeant gathered, did not like it one bit. The machinery of the law ground slowly into action. Police officers of progressively increasing seniority, and civilians of like expertise, were fetched from their firesides or, later, from their beds. Police cars shuttled up and down between the police building and the lane. A preliminary search of the woods was carried out. At least one of Gerry Reynolds' pheasants was dazzled by a police lantern and vanished into the boot of a panda car. As Keith had predicted, the lurking police-cars near the road-junctions were turned into full-scale road-blocks.

Through all this activity Sir Peter's Daimler purred sedately to and fro. Sir Peter and the car were too well-known to be suspected of anything, and the story of a fox-control operation was accepted without question. The Daimler visited Briesland House regularly, but there was never any further sign of occupation.

While all this was happening close to Newton Lauder, there was clandestine activity high up on the hill. Gerry Reynolds' cottage was visited, via the main road, by Archie Curran and Hughie Spence. Mary Bruce went there too.

Church bells were calling the faithful, and anyone else whom it might concern, to early Communion in the Episcopal Church when Sir Peter and his three recruits arrived at the flat over the gun-shop the following morning. Despite the early hour Keith was up, bright-eyed and active, sitting over coffee and the debris of a hearty breakfast. Also on the table were the telephone, several directories, a map and some small piles of paper, heavily scribbled on in Keith's neat fist.

'I got the note,' Keith said.

Not without a little self-conscious pride, Sir Peter laid three envelopes on the table. John Galloway had affected a heavy, Italic script with a broad nib and black ink, and it was clearly his hand that had marked the envelopes. The first said '5,000 x £10', the second '2,700 x £20' and the third '610 x £100'.

'They were under the hatch to the transmission-brake,' Ronnie said proudly. 'There's others of us can think, beside yourself.'

Molly put out more coffee, and the group settled round the table. 'Keith's been up again since around four, and phoning people,' Molly said. 'Would you believe it?' She spoke with quiet pride in Keith's eccentricity.

'On a Sunday morning?'

'I'm a popular lad today all right,' Keith said. 'There's

folk all over Scotland sticking pins in little wax effigies of me for spoiling their lie-ins, but I got what I wanted.'

'And what did you want?' Janet asked.

'First off, I wanted the use of Ralph Enterkin's office for the day.'

'You called Mr Enterkin and got him out of bed in the small hours of the Sabbath?' Molly asked incredulously. The solicitor, a noted *bon viveur*, was not known for his eager rising to greet the dawn.

Keith nodded cheerfully. 'He said he'd sue me, but he's in his office now, clearing the more confidential papers out of the way. It was the only place I could borrow in a hurry with more than one telephone-line. And Jake Paterson's in his shop, making a special gadget for me. And I fixed it with John Giulianotti for the ice-cream van.'

'Giulianotti?' said Hamish. 'That the mannie that won the down-the-line competition last month?'

'That's him.'

'Never mind that,' Ronnie said impatiently. He protruded his formidable jaw. 'What the hell is all this about offices and telephones and gadgets and ice-cream vans?'

Keith sighed. 'But I explained all that last night. Didn't you take it in?'

'You thought you explained,' Sir Peter said gently, 'but you fell asleep.'

'Did I? I thought I remembered delivering quite a lecture on it. Anyway, it's obvious, isn't it?'

'No,' said everybody, in tones ranging from curiosity to anger.

'Oh!' Keith scratched the back of his neck.

'Go over it from the beginning,' said Sir Peter. 'Summarise.'

'There are rewards going begging,' Keith said obediently, 'on a parcel of jewels and some money. The jewels have been split into two lots. Half is mingled with Noddy Chalmers, and as long as the local fuzz are hopping all over the place like fleas on a blanket there's not a lot that we or anybody else can do to find or move him. Stalemate. The other half's gone adrift from Noddy's motor-bike, and while I have my ideas about that I can't think of anything constructive to do about it for the moment.

'But there's also the money. We now know that our surmise was right. Danny Bruce has the notes, but we have one number or part of a number out of each. Right?'

'Last three digits,' Sir Peter said.

'If we can bring them together we're in for ten per cent. of a hundred and . . .' Keith jotted on a scrap of paper '. . . sixty-five thousand quid. My share and Molly's would be over six-and-a-half thousand, and that isn't the sort of money I leave lying if I drop it in the street. What's more, today's the day for doing something about it.

'So we're going to phone Danny Bruce and offer to swap half the numbers that we've got for half the notes that he's got. We don't let him know who we are, of course.'

'But we want the reward on all of it,' Ronnie pointed out.

'Of course you do, my little fellow,' Keith said, 'and so do I, and God willing we shall have it. Cinderella *shall* go to the World Cup, and we'll buy Briesland House and live happily ever after.'

'I want to surface the drive,' Sir Peter said wistfully, 'and put a couple of bathrooms into the place up north.'

'But first,' Keith said firmly, 'we have to see that Danny Bruce is caught with the money on him, either by us or by the police. He's a cautious and slippery sod, and you can bet your boots the notes aren't in his house. He'll have them stowed in a safe-deposit, or in one of the hideaways that Cathcart told me about. So we make sure that he has the notes in his sweaty paw, and keep him talking on the phone for a long time. And can you think of any other vehicle that can drive round and round the streets of Glasgow making a loud and distinctive noise?'

There was a gloomy silence. Nobody wanted to be the first to sound pessimistic, because Keith with his blood up could be a devastating critic of his detractors.

'Hell of a lot of streets in Glasgow,' Ronnie said at last.

'And quite a lot of time to play with. But given a little luck I hope to be able to home you in quicker than that. You can always hear some background noises over the phone. It's bad enough that the G.P.O.'s considering changing to a new pattern of microphone.'

'You won't hear much if it's a bad line,' said Molly.

'That's if you're calling next door,' Keith said. 'I had a call from the States last week. I could hear a dog barking and cars going by.'

Sir Peter was nodding. 'It might work,' he said. 'Ledbetter kept me hanging on the phone last week and I could hear everything that went on. You came in, Hamish, and took five gallons and a pint of oil, and ordered some paraffin for the brooders.'

'Well, I don't like it one damn bit,' Ronnie said with his usual belligerence. 'I say we arrange to meet him and swap. Two cars draw up, window-to-window, but we all hide in the back and jump him.'

'It may come to that,' Keith said. 'But suppose he's thought of it first. That's two cars full of men, presumably armed. Can you think of a better recipe for disaster?'

'That's not on,' Molly said. 'Keith, you're not going on any trip like that!'

'Calm down,' Keith said. 'I'm planning so that the need for a real meeting doesn't arise. We've got to have him on the phone for several hours anyway, because you can't just swap half the notes for half the numbers. They've got to match. So we may as well make the most use of that period.'

'Over eight thousand numbers,' Sir Peter said, scribbling. 'At five seconds each, twelve to the minute, I make it more than eleven hours.'

'Not that long,' said Keith. 'The danger is that he says, "You take the tens and I'll take the twenties and we'll split the hundreds".'

'About an hour,' Sir Peter said, scribbling again. 'No, less than that because they don't all have to be read out.'

'But if we refuse to take hundred-pound notes we get longer, and we can spin it out with breaks and distractions. So what do you think? Is the chance worth the effort?'

Sir Peter looked round the group. 'You've worked the oracle before,' he said. 'I think we'll go along with you again.'

Hamish nodded vigorously. For years he had cherished the notion of buying a croft in preparation for either marriage or retirement, whichever came first. Ronnie hesitated and then shrugged.

'Just give me the one day,' Keith said. 'If we haven't scored by tonight, you can make up your mind whether you want to forget it, or tell Munro all about it and hope for the best, or meet Danny Bruce and hope that he isn't matching our moves.'

'No confrontations,' Molly said. 'Do the watching and thinking, but let the police do any strong-arm stuff.'

'I've just had a thought,' said Janet proudly. 'If we don't want two carloads of people shooting it out, why not set up a meet with motor-bikes? You can't hide a man on a pillion. Then our man just pulls out a gun.'

'Fine,' said Keith, 'if you'll just guarantee me that Danny

Bruce's man won't have come along without any money, intending to pull his gun out first.'

'Then why don't we send one man on a motor-bike, and follow it up with the rest of us in a car, with guns?'

'Same answer. You've got to remember that Danny Bruce is tricky and careful. He doesn't go in for acts of violence himself, but he's got the means and the resources to hire plenty of others to be violent on his behalf. No, if we meet him at all it has to be on a better footing than that. Any ideas that will work even if Danny Bruce has the identical brainwave?'

The others looked at each other uneasily. ' 'Fraid not,' Janet said.

'Right,' Keith said briskly. 'So much for democracy and direct action. We try the subtle way first. Now, Molly and Janet stay with me and the rest of you beat it to Glasgow. Take pencils and paper. Go to George Square, the Tourist Information place, and get all the maps, guides and brochures that they've got. Then pick up the ice-cream van and phone me. I've written down the address of the van and both of Enterkin's phone-numbers.

'One more thing,' he added. 'We had ten per cent of the reward – one per cent of the gross – uncommitted. I want to promise Jake Paterson half of it, and to have your agreement to commit the rest if need be? Is that all right?'

'We trust you,' Sir Peter said simply.

'Thanks. Now, get going before the police arrive.'

'The police? Why should they – ?'

'Because now that they've found the second body they'll start to believe in the first one. And when that happens they'll want lots and lots of statements from Molly and me, and we'll have to tell all. After that, we're sitting on the side-lines and watching the game. That's why we move today, now. If we had more time we could set up a better operation, but we haven't. Synchronise watches, and away with you.'

Fifty yards down and across the square and two flights up, Jacob Paterson was already at work in Mr Enterkin's office. Keith, Molly and Janet made their way there by devious back lanes and closes.

Jake was the sole and unlikely fruit of a marriage between an immigrant Jewess and a Glasgow-Irish labourer. He had opted out of a career in computer engineering for the more peaceful and lucrative life as proprietor of Newton Lauder's only radio and television shop, but his natural genius for all things electronic kept him much in demand as occasional consultant to small firms all over Europe. His appearance was as startling as his aptitude, for he had inherited his mother's nose and his father's flaming red hair, both of which were still considered to be among the sights of Dennistoun.

Keith locked the entry door at ground floor level, and when they were in Mr Enterkin's outer office he locked that door too. He then unbagged and loaded his repeating shotgun.

Jake watched him from the door to the inner office. 'Preparing for a siege?' he asked. 'Not that I mind, but it's nice to know.'

'We're preparing,' Keith said grimly, 'to try and separate a crook from his money by tracking him down over the phone. He may have people trying to track us down in a wee while. On top of that, there's two other men don't like us over-much. Our only advantage is advance knowledge and being prepared. So I don't know about you, but prepared is what I'm going to be.'

Mr Enterkin's office comprised two rooms, an outer

office for his fat and friendly secretary-telephonist-typist and an inner sanctum. The outer office was a model of business efficiency and tidiness; the sanctum usually resembled a municipal dump, but due either to Keith's persuasiveness or to an unusual burst of energy on Mr Enterkin's behalf, the desk and table were swept clear and the mounds of papers had been restacked in the corners.

From his shop, Jake Paterson had brought a large hi-fi unit and it stood, half-dismantled, on Mr Enterkin's side-table. Its intestines, usually secret, spilled over the surface of the table and were supplemented by a number of additional components attached by wires and clips. It looked like space-age garbage. Four large speakers were relaying the sound of the speaking clock.

'Crikey!' Janet said. 'I thought she was in the room.'

Jake shrugged. His mother's blood made the gesture expressive. 'I can almost but not quite give you quadrophonic.' He made a tiny adjustment to a variable condenser. 'I only intended to use the amplifier and speakers, but I tried the Dolby unit as well, to see if it could wash out the background fuzz. And it did.'

'It's superb,' Keith said. 'We're almost home and dry.'

'The speaking clock's easy,' Jake said. 'It's coming straight off a good recording. But when you're hooked to a telephone at the other end you'll be stuck with a small microphone and a narrow wave-band of sound.'

'H'm,' Keith said. 'Which phone are you taking this off?'

'The one next door.'

'And you can tape from it as well?'

'No problem. But I couldn't play it back without losing the next bit.'

'That's what I thought,' Keith said. 'We need another machine, plus an extra one again, and earphones.'

'Easy enough. I've got a shop full of that sort of gear. But what's the last one for?'

Keith sat down in the swivel-chair behind the desk and spun himself around. 'A man as cautious as Danny Bruce won't give us his secret number, he'll want to call us. That will tell him what town we're in. If we can try to use background noise to find him, he might think of doing the same. So just in case we hear musical car-horns outside let's have some taped noises to confuse him. What could you produce?'

'There's a record of vintage cars in the shop,' Jake said thoughtfully, 'and a tape of a show with farmyard noises.'

'Keep it probable,' Molly said. 'I mean, if Danny Bruce hears the mating call of the killer whale, he's going to wonder. Or even an aircraft going over, because the map would tell him that Newton Lauder's miles off any flight-path. It might be the purest coincidence that we heard an ice-cream van or something, but if we play him a recording of charging elephants he's going to think, "They're trying to confuse me. I wonder why".'

'Good point,' Keith said. 'Keep it probable, Jake, and you've got an hour. Lock both doors both ways.'

Jake paused on the way out and cocked his head to listen to the voice of the speaking clock. 'If you turn the volume up and listen carefully,' he said, 'whenever she says "and twenty seconds" you can hear a tiny rustle of clothing.'

'Yes, yes,' Keith said. 'Very good. You're a clever lad. Well done. Now –'

'All right,' Jake said. 'I'm going. And I'll lock the door –'

'*Both* doors!'

'–both doors, both ways.'

Keith was left with the two girls, his small, dark wife and the taller, fair Janet. At another time the combination might have put ideas into his receptive head, if not of sex then of exquisite games of flirtation and jealousies and reconciliations. 'We want a voice,' he said. 'Just in case of reprisals or trickery, let's have a voice that won't be traced. Danny Bruce knows my voice, and he knows by now that I have an involvement in this so he may think of Molly. Janet, can you do a disguised voice?'

Janet started to shake her head. 'Wait a minute,' she said. 'At school I sometimes used to do a very posh, toffee-nosed English voice. A bit like Joyce Grenfell. Would that do?'

'Could you keep it up for hours, if you had to?'

'Oh yes. The more you do it, the harder it is to go back to your own voice.'

'Give me some numbers.'

Janet cleared her throat and looked up at Mr Enterkin's dusty ceiling. 'Right-oh. Jolly hockey-sticks.' Janet rattled off local telephone-numbers in a voice that became progressively more Girton.

'Now read some of these messages. You can paraphrase.'

Janet took a handful of Keith's paper slips. 'Certainly, darling. "Mr Bruce, I'm told that you're terribly interested in numbers. Little paper numbers, rather a lot of them. Fifty per cent, Mr Bruce. No, we've already been offered forty by Frank Hutch..."'

'That should make him light up and say "Tilt",' Keith said with satisfaction. 'Now pop through to next door, shut the door and practise loudly until I'm ready for the next stage.'

'With pleasure, my dear.'

'What do I do?' Molly asked.

'When we get going, you sit and log every background noise that you can hear, with the exact time and the number on the tape-counter. For the moment just hang on while I make a couple of phone-calls.' While he spoke, Keith was listening for Janet's voice. It was barely audible. He estimated that the solid old building was as nearly soundproof as he needed.

Keith found Inspector Cathcart's number in his diary and dialled it. He was quite prepared to try a dozen numbers before obtaining the inspector's home number, but to his surprise Cathcart answered at the second ring.

Keith identified himself. 'You work a long week, Inspector.'

'With people the way they are, I have to.'

'Are you still prepared to be helpful?'

'Until Superintendent Gilchrist tells me to stop. Or until I think you're coming it a bit.'

'Would you like to catch Danny Bruce in possession of money that could be proved to come from the resale of stolen goods?'

'Yes.' Cathcart sounded cautious.

'Archie Curran's in this too, and I might be able to hand him to you on a plate. And, finally, we're chasing a reward. There's an uncommitted share that might run as high as eight hundred or a thousand quid. I could promise, if we get the reward, to make a donation of that share to your favourite charity or police benevolent fund or whatever you like. Does that package buy some real help?'

There was a pause. Keith sweated. When Cathcart spoke, his voice had thawed considerably. 'It certainly does,' he said.

'About Archie Curran. You said you'd like to get him. Before he killed. "Again", you said.'

'Off the record?'

'Absolutely.'

'Mr Calder, that man killed a close friend of mine, a colleague who was doing no more nor less than his duty at the time. I know it, but we failed to convince a jury beyond reasonable doubt. Curran's been boasting of it ever since, but he can't be tried again. If there's just the least chance in the world of nailing Curran I'll give you all the help you can think of, provided only that I can do it within the book of rules.'

Keith wondered how strictly Cathcart would interpret the rule-book. 'For starters,' he said, 'do you know any of Danny Bruce's current addresses, the rooms or flats in Glasgow that he uses?'

Cathcart thought for a moment. 'I'll see what I can do and call you back.'

Keith felt more relaxed. Cathcart's rule-book might not be too stringent. He gave Cathcart Mr Enterkin's two phone-numbers. 'If we get Danny Bruce on the phone and he's got the money with him, could you get the call traced?'

'On a Sunday? I can try. It depends who I can get hold of. If I'd known yesterday . . .'

'If we can get an unlisted call-back number out of him, could you get the address?'

'Same answer. I can try, that's all.'

'Nobody can do more,' Keith said. 'What kind of car does Danny Bruce drive?'

'Sometimes he hires. Rest of the time he uses taxis and public transport, and he doesn't mind walking.'

'I see. How much of today can you be available?'

For the first time Cathcart's voice was amused. 'Mr

Calder, I'm a dedicated bachelor. Dedicated to my job, I mean, not to non-marriage. I was just about to go home and sit wondering what the hell to do next on a dull Sabbath in Glasgow. I can be available all day and all night.'

'If we can get him to leave home, heading for where he's got the money hidden, could you follow Danny Bruce?'

Clearly over the line, against the background of a distant typewriter, Keith could hear Cathcart's sigh. 'Mr Calder, I've already told you about Danny Bruce and now you want me to shadow him at ten minutes' notice on a Sunday. Try to understand. For a man like Bruce who always, as a matter of habit, ducks through alleys and goes home if he sees the same face twice, you need a big team. I'd want two plain cars and six men on foot, all with radios, before I'd even try it. And then I wouldn't be optimistic, not on the Sabbath with the streets empty. And the way we're manned these days I could no more put my hand on a team like that today than fly in the air. The off-duty men will be scattered all over Scotland by now.'

'Well,' Keith said, 'if you can't you can't.'

'That's the way of it. Why can you not do it in a couple of days' time?'

This was the question that Keith had most feared. He could hardly explain that he distrusted Cathcart's colleague Munro and was avoiding for as long as possible giving him a statement in a matter of murder. 'Bruce will believe the story that we've got for him just now,' he said. 'In a day or two his daughter will have given him a full briefing and he'll guess who we are and what we're after.'

'I see,' Cathcart said. He sounded unconvinced. 'You'd better explain the set-up to me.'

Keith gave him a brief and edited explanation of the embezzled money and its connection with the stolen gems. He stressed that the bank-notes were in Glasgow. He explained that the jewels were still unfound, suggesting, without quite saying, that the police in Newton Lauder had that matter well in hand. Inspector Cathcart, when he rang off, sounded as satisfied as, in Keith's experience, any policeman ever did; but Keith's experiences with the police had rarely produced much satisfaction for either side.

Keith sat looking at the dead telephone. 'Funny,' he said. 'I'm trusting him more than I would Munro. Maybe it's because I've never met him.'

Molly had been thinking along her own lines. 'If somebody has to meet Danny Bruce – and please God don't let it be you! – why not do the swap absolutely straight and have Inspector Cathcart pick up Danny Bruce on the way back?'

'Who knows which way he'd come back? If it was me, I'd pick a place in between a dozen junctions. He might even put the numbers straight into an envelope and pop them in a post-box. Anyway, he'd only have been carrying half of the bank-notes, and we might never get a sniff of the other half.'

TWELVE

By the time that Jake Paterson returned, grumbling under the weight of two tape-players, an oscilloscope and a miscellany of other equipment, Keith, with the aid of the girls, had scripted every turn of argument with Danny Bruce that they could conceive of and had coached Janet in such improvisations as she might have to make.

'There were two bobbies at your door,' Jake said.

'What did they want?'

'Didn't ask.'

'Pity. I'd have liked to know whether they were after us with questions or just wanting to return another lost pistol. Now, let's make the first call.'

'The others haven't called in from Glasgow yet,' Molly objected.

'And I don't want them selling fags all over Glasgow if we can't reach Danny Bruce. Let's have a trial run.'

'I've got butterflies in my little tum,' Janet said, but she sat down at the secretary's desk, spread out Keith's slips of paper on its plastic top and, before she could lose her nerve, dialled quickly.

Danny Bruce was at home and answered the phone himself. As Jake had predicted, the quality of sound was diminished by the small and narrow-band microphone, but the rich, fruity voice with its faint overtone of the better parts of Glasgow came through with a clarity that conjured up for Keith the man himself – heavily fleshed, dark-jowled and prosperous-looking. Jake made another tiny adjustment to one of his condensers and turned the volume up a touch, and Keith suddenly realised that he could hear Danny Bruce's watch ticking through seventy miles of wire.

Janet, alone in the outer office, was word-perfect in the messages that they had revised and rehearsed. 'Mr Bruce, you don't know me but I know you.'

Danny Bruce sounded amused. 'What shall I call you, then?'

'Call me Cynthia,' Janet said in her very best accent.

'As good a name as any other,' Bruce agreed.

'Mr Bruce, I believe that you might be interested in some numbers.'

'Numbers?'

'Little paper numbers. Lots and lots of them. Are you interested?'

'I could be.'

'Either you are or you aren't. It's up to you.'

'All right, then,' Bruce said slowly. 'Take it that I'm interested.'

'Well, Mr Bruce, I have the numbers and you have the notes. Neither is any use without the other. I suggest that we get together and that I give you half the numbers and you give me half the notes.'

'I see . . . This will bear discussion. But not on this line. I'll call you in an hour. What number?'

'This phone isn't as secure as I'd like,' Janet said. 'Can I phone you?'

'No you can not,' Bruce said sharply. 'I phone you, or the deal's off.'

Janet paused deliberately, as if in hesitation, before answering and then gave the number.

'Right,' said Bruce. 'One hour.' And he hung up.

Janet came and opened the door. 'He's not going to be

easy,' she said. Her voice was still Cheltenham and Oxford.

'He's not going to be impossible either,' Keith said. 'You were good, by the way.'

'I believe Keith's actually enjoying all this,' Jake said.

'He is,' said Molly. 'There's nothing that he enjoys as much as a challenge and a battle of wits.' The inner office phone rang. 'That'll be Sir Peter.'

Keith lifted the receiver. It was Inspector Cathcart with two addresses known to have been used by Danny Bruce in recent months. 'I'm making no headway with the Post Office Telecommunications people,' he added, 'but I'll persevere.'

'We've got other ways and means,' Keith said, 'but a trace would be quickest and most certain. It'll be a call from Glasgow to the other phone,' he gave the number, 'and it'll be made at about eleven-fifty.'

'I'll keep trying. Any other day but Sunday . . . And I'll have to clear this with your local police.'

Inside himself, Keith cringed. 'Of course you must,' he said blandly. 'But if you do it before we've secured the money you'll be sure to lose half of your share of the reward to their funds. As it is, I'm sure you'll have nearly a thousand quid coming.'

'And,' Cathcart said, 'if anybody knew that I'd held back from proper procedure for a reason like that I could find myself alongside Danny Bruce – in deep trouble.'

'Do you know Chief Inspector Munro at Newton Lauder?'

'We've met. A very thorough man.'

Cathcart's tone gave Keith the clue that he needed. 'Yes, he's thorough and meticulous. But he's also slow and cautious, and he does everything by that book of yours. If you bring him in too soon, he'll dilly and dally and insist on protocol until the fish has spat out the hook.'

'That's another reason I can't use, but it's a strong one. I'll hold off just yet a while. But I'm putting my head on the block. If you let the chopper fall, I'll follow you around for the rest of my life with a suitcase full of blank summonses.' He disconnected.

Keith allowed himself a moment for a quick shudder. Cathcart had sounded sincere. 'Right,' Keith said, 'let's listen to the tape.'

They listened in silence to the short conversation. 'From now on, Molly,' Keith said, 'you'd better log all pauses, with time and tape-counter number. Now, what have we learned?'

'Nothing of any use,' Janet said. 'A door slammed. Big deal!'

'A glass door,' Molly said. 'The glass sounded loose.'

'Children's voices,' said Jake. 'Does Danny Bruce have children?'

'Only his daughter, and she's in her late twenties,' Keith said. 'They'll be next door's bairns. Jake, play the tape again.' Jake played the tape. 'What's the thumping sound?'

'Somebody banging his head against a brick wall,' Janet said disgustedly. 'Just the same as we're doing.'

Jake laughed. 'Rubbish,' he said. 'I'll tell you what it was – a ball being bounced against a wall.'

Molly was looking depressed. 'Suppose that that was the place that we were looking for. We couldn't tour Glasgow looking for a house with loose glass in the door and children playing with a ball.'

Keith refused to appear downcast. 'For a one-minute chat with a man who lives in a quiet street,' he said, 'that wasn't bad at all. But I hope to God the place he phones from's in a noisier area.'

'He said an hour. Does that give us a clue how far he has to travel?'

'It would,' Keith said, 'if we knew that he was leaving immediately, and how he was travelling, and if he was going anywhere first.'

'We should have had somebody waiting to follow him,' Molly said.

'If he's too canny for the police to follow then he's too good for us.' Keith spread a map of Glasgow over Mr Enterkin's desk and ringed the two addresses that Inspector Cathcart had given him.

When the phone rang again, it was Sir Peter. 'Here we are, then. Not so cold over this side.'

'A pity,' Keith said. 'If it stayed frosty, sound would travel better.'

'Have to do the best we can. We've got the van, and we're pulled up at a phone-box in Cathedral Street. There's a queue forming already. Ronnie looks fed up to the teeth but he's serving them.'

'Good. Make sure you always have plenty of change in the car. You can switch places, but from now on we want one driving the van and serving, one sitting beside him and logging your locations and times and any noises heard so that we can back-track, and one in the car tagging along and phoning me at every possible chance.'

'I've got that. I'll brief the others. And I've got the list of chimes here. We're playing "Daisy Bell" at the moment.'

'Too common. What else have you got?'

'How about Von Suppé "Light Cavalry"?'

'Much better. That'll only be used for gymkhanas and such. And I've got two possible addresses. Berkeley Street and Kersland Street. Get out near one of them and call me back from as close as you can.'

'Right. We were having a discussion on the way through,' Sir Peter said apologetically. 'Ronnie feels strongly –'

'I never knew him feel any other way,' Keith said.

'Quite so. But he doesn't think that we're going to win this one. He thinks we should meet Danny Bruce and do the swap, and have your friend Cathcart waiting to arrest him on the way back.'

Keith looked at his watch. Time was too short for him to say all that he would have liked. 'Molly just suggested that,' he said patiently. 'Please ask Ronnie, very politely, why Danny Bruce shouldn't post the numbers back to himself as soon as he's got them, and how Ronnie would know the route Bruce would take back, and how he'd prevent the handover developing into a shoot-out that would make the O.K. Corral look like a darts match. No, try it my way first.' They disconnected.

Keith snapped his fingers. 'We don't want another phone ringing in the background while we're talking. Jake, could you take the bell off this phone?'

'No problem. Pass the screwdriver.'

Keith started to pace the room. 'Can anybody think of anything else I've forgotten?'

'Calm down,' Molly said. 'You're the one who always tells me not to worry.'

Keith stopped in his stride. 'I don't believe in worrying when there's not a damn thing you can do about it. That's contingency worrying. But when it may produce something useful, then it's constructive worrying and I'm all for it.' He started pacing again. 'If I'd timed it better, we might have had church bells. I hope the bastard hasn't heard of double-glazing.'

Molly sighed. 'Not in a rented room,' she said. 'Anyway, that's not constructive.'

The next call on the sanctum phone produced no more than a muted buzz. 'That what you wanted?' Jake asked.

'Fine.' Keith picked up the receiver. The voice was strange. 'Who's that?'

'It's me. Hamish.' The telephone line brought out a Borders accent in Hamish's voice which Keith had never noticed before.

'Where's Sir Peter?'

'In the van. He couldn't read my writing, so we swapped jobs. We're in Sauchiehall Street, near Berkeley Street.'

'Sir Peter might be a better salesman than Ronnie.'

Hamish laughed shortly. 'Are you sure Ronnie can write? Listen, we've been discussing.'

Keith suppressed a sigh. 'Go ahead,' he said.

'Why don't we arrange the meet and nail him on the way there?' Hamish said. 'We know where's he's starting from. Why don't we catch him outside his house?'

'Because we don't know whether he'd leave the house with the money or pick it up along the way. And because if he brings any money at all it would only be half.'

'I see,' Hamish said.

'Well, explain it to Ronnie, in words of one syllable or less. I think he only understands grunts. Don't stop thinking, because we may need all the ideas we can get, but you'll have to do better than that. Hold on, now. We should be away shortly. When I give the word, go through Berkeley Street and Kersland Street, dinging all the way.'

'Right. Don't be longer than you have to,' Hamish said. 'The queue's building up, and Ronnie looks fit to bust.'

'Let him bust if he wants to,' Keith said.

Minutes later, the phone rang in the outer office.

'Is that – er – Cynthia?' Danny Bruce's voice said over the speakers.

'Go,' Keith said into the other phone, and he hung up. He half-opened the door between the two rooms so that he could hear the loudspeakers and still remain in touch with Janet.

'Is my daughter all right?' Danny Bruce was saying.

Janet looked up at Keith, who nodded. 'She was in good shape when last seen,' Janet said, 'which was yesterday morning. If we see her, shall we remind her to phone home?'

'She can look after herself,' Bruce said, but he sounded worried. 'How do I know that you don't have her?'

'If we had her,' Janet said calmly, 'would we be offering you a fifty-fifty split of the money? For your daughter's life, I'm sure you'd come down another one per cent . . .' She raised her eyebrows and Keith gave her a thumbs-up signal.

'All right,' said Bruce. 'So you've only got the numbers. But that's my money. Why should I give you half?'

'You don't have to,' Janet said. She picked up a note. 'I can always sell the numbers to Frank Hutch. And it's not your money, it's anybody's money. First it was embezzled. Then it was paid over for stolen goods. And, finally, your client never got delivery of the goodies. You're lucky to get half of it.'

'You know a lot,' Bruce said, and the line was so clear that Keith could almost hear him frown. 'You might as well tell me who you are.'

'And I might just as well not,' Janet said firmly.

There was a moment's silence at the other end. 'You

169

wouldn't have the gems, by any chance, would you?'
Danny Bruce said. 'If you have, I'll still give you a good
price for them.'

'Better than ten per cent of the insured value?'

'Certainly,' said Bruce. His voice lacked enthusiasm.

'We'll bear it in mind,' Janet said. 'But let's go on
about the money.' She picked up another of Keith's notes.
'I suggest that we meet and do an exchange.'

'Agreed,' said Bruce. 'Two cars, door to door. Only
one person in each or I drive straight on.'

Janet switched to another slip of paper. 'My only con-
dition,' she said, 'is that I don't want any hundreds. I have
no connection for passing them. I want money that I can
spend.'

'How like a woman,' said Danny Bruce. There was a
pause. Keith crossed his fingers and prayed. 'Agreed,'
said Bruce's voice.

'Got him,' Keith mouthed.

'In turn,' said Bruce, 'I choose the place.'

'Very well.'

'At the agreed time, you start from Melbourne and drive
west on the A721 towards Carluke. We meet where we
meet.'

Keith grunted. From memory, the first ten miles or so
of that road had nearly twenty junctions.

'What will you be driving?' Janet asked.

'I'll flash you,' Bruce said. 'You tell me what car.'

'I'll phone you at the last moment and tell you.'

Danny Bruce chuckled. 'You're nobody's fool, are you,
my dear? When this is over, we must have a talk. All right,
you phone me at the last moment. When is it going to be?'

'It must be quick,' Janet said. 'Make it seven tomorrow
morning.'

'Why the hurry?'

'Because my partner wants to sell to Frank Hutch. He thinks he can buy himself into a share of the jewels that way.'

'Do you think Hutch has got the jewels?' Bruce asked.

'No.'

'And you think you can keep all of your half of the money, and leave your partner out in the cold? Very understandable.' Danny Bruce chuckled again, fatly. He was in familiar territory. 'All right. Seven tomorrow morning it is. If you don't phone me by six to describe your car I'll know that your partner was too quick for you and I'll go back to bed and watch the newspapers. But this will never do, I'll be giving you cold feet. Which numbers are you going to bring?'

Janet flashed a quick smile at Keith and gave him back his thumbs-up sign. 'How do you mean?' she asked innocently.

'I suggest,' Bruce said patiently, 'that I take the hundreds, you take the tens and we divide the twenties.'

'Agreed,' said Janet.

'Just a moment.' There was silence on the line.

'Are you taping all this?' Keith asked Jake.

'Every whisper.'

'On that basis,' Bruce's voice came back, 'I'm due twenty-three and a half thousand pounds out of the twenties.'

'Twenty-one and a half,' said Janet. She winked at Keith.

'Of course,' Bruce said quickly. 'My mistake. But the numbers have to match. It's no use your handing me the numbers from one thousand and seventy-five twenties. I've got to have the numbers that match the notes that I've kept.'

'Ah yes,' said Janet. She sounded surprised and dismayed. Keith thought that, if life on the farm was not for her, she might well have a future on the stage. 'And *vice versa*, of course.'

'This is going to take several hours,' Bruce said. 'I suggest that you read to me the numbers of the twenties that you're going to give me.'

Janet looked at Keith. He reached the desk in three quick strides and sorted one of his notes out of the bottom of what was becoming a ragged pile. Janet nodded. 'The numbers are all muddled together,' she said. 'It'll take me hours to sort out the different denominations, and all night to sort the numbers. You'd better read to me.'

'All right,' said Bruce, and Keith uttered a silent shout of rejoicing. So Bruce had the money with him. 'I'll read to you. I'll read out the numbers that you will bring to me. You understand?'

'I quite understand, Mr Bruce,' Janet said. She sounded like the better sort of duchess. 'I bring you the numbers from all the hundreds, plus the numbers that you're going to read out from the twenties. You bring me all the ten-notes plus the notes whose numbers you haven't read out.'

'You've got it, my dear. Shall we start?'

'Hang on a moment. I've got a pen and a letter-pad in my bag.' Janet got up, stretched and walked across to Keith. She looked at Molly's back. She rubbed noses with Keith and walked back to the secretary's desk. 'I'm ready,' she said.

Danny Bruce started reading numbers.

When Danny Bruce's call had first come through, Keith, for a heart-stopping moment, had been unable to hear any background noise at all; then as his ears attuned he had begun to hear traffic noises and a bicycle bell. Replayed at higher volume, the tapes might be more informative.

Keith went back into Mr Enterkin's sanctum and looked over Molly's shoulder. Her list was longer than he had dared to hope. Jake, too, was making notes. Keith changed the cassette and took it with the first pages of Molly's notes to where Jake was sitting. 'See what you can make out of this,' he said.

Jake nodded, and put on earphones.

The phone was buzzing softly and Keith picked it up. 'Hamish? You took a hell of a time for a mile-and-a-half run.'

'The police held us up.'

'Oh God! Speeding?'

'Two cones and a packet of Benson and Hedges. Did you hear us?'

'Afraid not.' Keith was studying Molly's notes, but they confirmed his own recollection. 'We heard a van go by playing "William Tell". If you meet him, ask him where he was at eleven twenty-five. He won't know, but ask him anyway.'

'Have you arranged a meeting-place with Bruce yet?' Hamish asked.

'Yes. A country road with about twenty junctions on it.'

'Couldn't you get him to change it? Say that you don't fancy anywhere so lonely, you want to meet him in a crowded place, say Queen Street Station at rush-hour. Then we could have your friend Callahan, or whatever his name is – '

'Cathcart.'

'Yes. He could be waiting to pounce.'

'We may have to try it,' Keith said, 'but I don't see Danny Bruce falling for a trick like that. Do you?'

173

'I suppose not,' Hamish said. 'It's getting warmer over here.'

'Maybe we're in for a thaw over this side,' Keith said. The faint shadow of an idea passed across the deepest recesses of his consciousness but it faded and was gone before he could examine it. 'Knock off for about ten minutes and call again.'

'I don't know that we can knock off, just like that. Every time we stop there's a queue of wifies with pudding-basins.'

'Don't stand any nonsense,' Keith said. 'Be bold, bloody and resolute.'

'Aye,' said Hamish. 'I'll be bold, and Sir Peter's resolute all right.'

'And Ronnie's being bloody as usual?'

'You can put that to music and play it on the pipes,' Hamish said.

Keith moved over to stand behind Jake Paterson. 'I spotted the buses,' he said, looking at Jake's notes. 'What's A.F.P.?'

'Ambulance, fire-engine or police-car. I wouldn't know what dings or whoops or goes hee-haw in Glasgow these days.'

'Nor would I,' said Keith. 'Next time Cathcart's on the phone we'll play it to him. If it's a fire-engine, the fire-master's office could help us. Are you sure about the train?'

'Ninety per cent.,' Jake said. 'It's distant, but played at high volume there's not much doubt about it. An electric train.'

'That's a help. What's this?'

'Just a buzzing. I want to play it over the oscilloscope when I get a minute.'

'And that's the lot?'

'You want miracles?'

174

Keith considered. 'Yes,' he said, 'that's just what I want. But this'll do for now. . . . There's the phone again.'

Inspector Cathcart was back on the line. He sounded depressed. The telephone supervisor had told him a few home-truths and they rankled. 'If I can't get hold of either her boss or mine soon,' he said, 'it's no good.'

'Keep trying,' Keith said, 'but first listen to this.' He caught Jake's attention and they played a few inches of tape over the phone. 'Now, what was that?'

'Ambulance.'

'You're sure it wasn't a fire-engine?'

'Certain.'

'Pity,' Keith said. 'That's the one service that does business as usual on a Sunday. One more question. Are Hughie Spence and Archie Curran in Glasgow, as of now?'

'I'll put the word around and let you know if anyone sees them,' Cathcart said. 'That's the best that I can do.' Even the small click as he hung up sounded dispirited.

Keith went back to Jake. 'Anything?'

'I think so. At least it's not a bluebottle in the room, which is what I thought at first. The oscilloscope shows a constant series of sharp, rapid pulses. It's a very small, high-speed internal combustion engine.'

'Chain-saw?'

'Not very likely in Glasgow on a Sunday.' Jake scratched his head. 'And there's a slight Doppler-shift on a seven-second cycle, as near as I can figure it. Trouble is, so much of it's obscured by voices.'

'Don't bug me with science,' Keith said. 'What *is* it?'

'I don't like guessing.'

'Go ahead and guess, if you want your five per cent . . .'

Jake shrugged. 'For my money, it's a model plane on a hand-line. But I'm not sure I'd bet on it.'

'You just did,' Keith said. 'Public park?'

175

'Or school playground. Or somebody with a large garden.'

'Don't make life difficult. We'll concentrate on the parks first. What else have you got?'

'You're a glutton. Give me the next tape and I'll see what I can get.'

One minute later the phone buzzed again. It was Ronnie on the line. 'They'll not let me do the selling any more,' he said disgustedly.

'What did you do?'

'Och well, it was just something that happened. Nothing at all, really.'

'What was it?' Keith demanded.

'We thought we'd get a quick snack while we weren't on the move, but there was folks at the van. I said we was closing for our own lunch, but one woman, a big, Italian-looking wifie with a colossal bust hanging half-out and a tunnel between like a badger's sett –'

'Stick to the story,' Keith said.

'I am. She said we was to serve her. She was first in the queue, she said, and if we didn't sell her some ice-cream she was going to report us to somebody-or-other.'

'My God,' Keith said, 'you didn't – ?'

'I bloody did! A whole scoopful right down the tunnel. Did you not hear her scream? It must've carried that far. The other women thought it was funny, though, so she's not well liked. I doubt it'll go any further.'

'If it does,' Keith said grimly, 'I'll fill you bung full of ice-cream through an enema-tube, you great pudding. From now on, behave yourself!'

'Och, it was a nothing. A nothing!' Ronnie sounded, for him, quite subdued.

'Listen now,' Keith said. 'Did you see an ambulance about eleven-thirty?'

There was a rustle of paper at the other end. 'No. Passed one later, though.'

'Never mind. The place we want is near a bus-route, so stick to bus-routes from now on. It's near a public park or similar open space, and not far from an electrified railway-line.'

'Now, how the hell would you know all that?'

'Waved my magic wand. I don't know which lines are electrified, but I'm sure the one out of Dumbarton is.' Keith was poring over the map while he spoke. 'You go to Victoria Park. Go once round, then come back and do Yorkhill Park. By that time I'll hope to know which lines are electric. Got it?'

'Got it.'

'If you get the chance – but don't waste time over it – stop at each park and ask whether anyone was flying a model plane on a hand-line between eleven-fifteen and eleven-thirty.'

Later, one of Keith's strongest memories of the day was of the distracting need to stop and explain to the others what the far end of a telephone conversation had been about. Now, when he wanted to phone Cathcart or to listen to the background noises or to consult Jake again, Molly and Jake were desperate to know how Ronnie had sinned. When Keith explained Molly was shocked, but Jake laughed until he cried.

'Everyone's gone to the moon,' Cathcart said despairingly when Keith called him, 'and there's a frustrated old biddy at the exchange who wants a personal say-so from God before she'll even tell me the time. I think her pram must have had a parking-ticket and she's never forgotten it. If you've got a number I could try and trace that.'

'No luck,' Keith said. 'But we're getting other clues.'

Can you tell me which Glasgow railway-lines are electrified?'

'Off-hand the Dumbarton line, the line south and the Circle. I could check and call you back. And, by the way, your two friends are still in Glasgow.'

'That's a relief,' Keith said. 'I don't think I could cope with any more complications just now. They don't seem happy and fulfilled, do they?'

'The reverse. One of my men spotted them, and he said that they looked like thunder. They were speaking to a shady dealer in the car trade, if it's any help.'

'That's what I wanted to know. They're probably trying to get a Land Rover.'

'I'll try to keep tabs on them,' Cathcart said. 'And if I don't call you back you'll know that I was right about the electrified lines. I'll have to go and get something to eat soon, but after that I'll stay by the phone.'

'Go now,' Keith said, 'but try not to be long. We may have something for you in a hurry.'

'Nothing else so far,' Jake said.

Keith could only bite his nails, until Molly stopped him, listen to the patient voice reading numbers and wait. Time limped by. The background noises of some Glasgow street were muted, partially obscured by interference on the line, half-covered by Danny Bruce's voice and as far as Keith could tell they could have come from anywhere in the city.

Ronnie phoned in from Ferry Road, near Yorkhill Park. 'Try Glasgow Green,' Keith said, and the connection was broken. 'I must have been bloody well nuts,' he said aloud. 'I should have had Cathcart in on this from the start. I should have phoned him last night. We're getting nowhere, and that's the only place – '

'Shut up a minute,' Jake said urgently.

They listened. Danny Bruce's voice recited numbers. Only the fact that they were the numbers of bank-notes, twenty pounds at a time, saved Keith from being driven mad. Not the least hint of 'Light Cavalry' came over the speakers.

'Didn't you hear it?'

'Whatever it was, no.'

'Ambulance,' said Jake. 'Another one. Not so near, this time. But it was getting nearer instead of going away, and it cut off at about the same volume as the other one. It may be coincidence. Or – '

'Hospital?'

'Could be.'

'That's what I thought,' said Molly.

'Come over here,' Keith told Jake. He gave him one of Mr Enterkin's pens. 'Make a ring round every hospital – '

Something thudded against the door. Molly opened it a crack and peeped through. 'Janet's signalling,' she whispered. 'She's holding up a clenched fist.'

'About twenty minutes left,' Keith said. 'We'd better have a break.' He looked at his watch. 'They should have cleared Glasgow Green in a minute.' He went softly into the outer office, sorted one of his notes out of the pile and laid it before Janet.

'Just a moment,' Janet said smoothly. 'I'm in trouble here. I can be seen at this phone, and I think one of Frank Hutch's boys is sniffing around. Give me a number to call back.'

Danny Bruce laughed. 'Put it out of your little mind,' he said. His voice was becoming hoarse. 'I'll go and have a snack. You phone my home in half an hour and leave

179

your new number with the cook. I'll phone you shortly after that.' He hung up without waiting for an answer.

'He's as canny as a whore in a nunnery,' Keith said. 'If I get my hands on him, he'll spend the rest of his life trying to grow a new pair of testicles. Well, we've bought some time.'

Janet came through from the other room. 'How did I do?' she asked. She sounded as if she had been opening a bazaar.

'Very good,' Keith said. 'You have a future as a confidence trickster.' He kissed her cheek and she glowed at him.

'If he's as canny as all that,' Molly said, 'mightn't he phone back from somewhere different next time?'

Keith swallowed. 'God forbid!' he said. 'We'd have to start all over again, with only twenty minutes to go. But it'd mean shifting the bank-notes, so he probably won't. Now, can I have some help marking up the map?'

'Before you do that,' said Jake, 'there's something else.'

THIRTEEN

Jake spun the tape back for a second and set it to play. 'If he'd just gone on talking for a few more moments,' he said irritably.

'Put it out of your little mind,' said Danny Bruce's rich voice. Jake turned up the volume. The voice paused before the last sentence. 'I'll phone you shortly after that,' it said, and they heard the receiver rattle and then a click and silence. Behind the voices and clearly in the brief pause a few melodious notes could be heard.

'Musical car-horn?' suggested Molly.

'Military band,' said Keith.

'Somebody turned up a radio?' Janet suggested.

'Possibly,' Jake said. 'What time did it start?'

Molly looked down at her log. 'The end of the call was just a few seconds after one.'

'The bands in the parks usually start at two, don't they?'

'There's no law says that they can't start earlier.' Keith had brought the Sunday paper with him, and he flicked over the pages until he found the radio and television programmes. 'Unless they've put on a brass band record as an entr'acte, I can't see anything.'

Janet was looking over Keith's shoulder, one breast deliberately nudging his cheek. 'Family Favourites?' she suggested.

Molly gave Janet a look which could have cut that young lady in half. 'Or somebody upstairs putting on a record,' she said.

'I'd go for that,' Keith said, 'except that Danny Bruce seemed to hang up in one hell of a hurry. Damn, damn,

damn!' He got up and started pacing the room again. 'We're back to shading probabilities. We'd already guessed public park, so a brass band adds to the likelihood – and to the time we'd waste going up a blind alley if we were wrong. We're pretty sure of the electric train, but we're only guessing that two ambulances suggest a hospital.'

'The point –' began Molly.

'The point is,' said Keith, 'that we've got to be looking somewhere. Hijacking him tomorrow morning would be a desperate last resort. And if we call on Cathcart and don't deliver the goods we'll have another policeman fed up at us. So. We've got limited time available and that means a limited area that we can cover. We'll plump for what we've got.'

He dialled Inspector Cathcart's number. There was no reply. 'I said he could go to lunch,' Keith said. 'Why do these blasted policemen have to listen to me?'

'They don't usually,' Molly said, giggling.

'That's what I mean, they pick the wrong times. Jake, we need to give him the other number. Can you swap everything around, room for room, quickly?'

Jake sighed and picked up his tools. 'Doesn't the time go quickly when you're working your arse off?' he said.

Molly looked up from the map. 'I've been marking hospitals and bandstands,' she said.

'Good girl! I suppose,' Keith said doubtfully, 'that there has to be a bandstand? Or do they just march up and down?'

'Bandstand, definitely,' said Jake looking up. 'This phone's trying to ring.'

The caller was Ronnie. 'Thank God!' Keith said. He peered at the map. 'We're looking for a park with a band playing. Did the tourist place give you anything that

182

would tell you whether any of the parks have a band playing today, starting at one o'clock?'

'The place in George Square was shut for the winter,' Ronnie said.

Keith withdrew his prayer of thanks and thought furiously. 'You've already eliminated Kelvingrove, and there's no hospital near Glasgow Green. Is the railway line that goes past Springburn Park and Stobhill Hospital electrified?'

'How would I know?' said Ronnie's voice. Jake and the two girls shook their heads in uncertainty.

Keith made up his mind. 'Tell the two in the van to go out to Springburn Park, see if there's a band playing and call me back on the other number. You take the Daimler and go down to Queen's Park. Danny Bruce is off the phone just now, so keep an eye out for him. He's about my height with a bit of a pot, always very well-dressed, usually a camel-hair coat out of doors. Silver hair, florid complexion, blue jaw unless he's freshly shaved, a nose that looks as if it may have been broken once and a wart beside his mouth, left side, I think.'

'Got it,' said Ronnie.

'Brief the others.'

They disconnected.

Jake was packing up his tools and the hi-fi equipment had disappeared. 'All swapped over,' he said.

'Including the bells?'

'Including the bells,' Jake said patiently.

Keith went through and dumped himself in the secretary's chair. The others drifted after him. 'We've a few minutes in hand,' Keith said. 'Maybe we can short-cut a bit.' He tried Cathcart's number again, without success. He took the Glasgow directory out of the desk and looked up Stobhill Hospital, dialled Glasgow and the Stobhill code and four digits at random.

'I'm hungry,' Molly said plaintively.

'Not long now.'

After a dozen rings, a voice came on at the other end.

'Are you near the park?' Keith asked.

'Who's this?' asked the voice.

'Are you near Springburn Park? *Please!*' Keith said.

'No' far. Who *is* this?'

'Do me a favour, mate. Listen out of the window and tell me if there's a band in the park.'

The receiver at the other end was ineffectively covered. Keith heard a voice, slightly muffled, say, 'C'mere, Kevin. There's a right nutter on the line.' The voice came back clearly, sounding amused. 'See here, Jimmy, is this some kind of a joke?'

'No joke,' Keith said. 'It's a matter of life and death. Is there a band in the park?'

'There wisnae when we came in jist now.'

Keith hung up. 'Queen's Park,' he said.

'Six-three-seven,' Jake said. 'I'd an auntie – '

'Still there?'

'Dead.'

'Sorry.' Keith waited a moment longer to allow for any incoming calls. Then he dialled Queen's Park and another random four-digit number. He got no answer. Frantic with impatience he tried another number and it answered on the second ring. The voice was female. Keith projected all his charm, all his sexual challenge into his voice. 'You live near Queen's Park, don't you?' he said.

'Aye, that's right,' the lady said coyly. 'Langside Avenue. Have we met?'

'Can you hear the band in the park?'

'Why, are they playing our tune?'

Keith ground his teeth, but he kept his voice insinuatingly virile. 'To win today's major prize,' he said, 'hum me the tune that the band's playing.'

The other receiver was laid down on a hard surface. Feet crossed a floor and a window squealed open. Faintly over the line came the strains of 'Poet and Peasant'. Keith hung up on the lady's attempt to hum the melody.

'Time you phoned the new number to Danny Bruce's house,' he told Janet, and she went back into the sanctum.

Keith dialled Cathcart's number. This time the inspector answered immediately.

'We're getting warm,' Keith said. 'It's an odds-on bet that Danny Bruce is within spitting distance of Queen's Park, and we know for sure that he's got the money in his hands. So this is where you come in. Can you get down there and call me back?'

'Yes, of course.'

Keith gave him the new number and rang off. 'I'm beginning to hate telephones,' he said. 'I seem to have spent all my life on this one, and yet when you want it to ring –'

The telephone gave an obliging buzz. Hamish was on the line. 'There's no band here,' he said.

'I guessed wrong,' Keith said. 'Get down to Queen's Park, quick.'

'It's about five miles!'

'In a straight line.'

'I'll be glad to get out of here,' Hamish said. 'There's a rival van-driver threatening a punch-up if we don't get off his pitch.'

'Get the hell off it, then,' Keith said, and disconnected. 'When people do this sort of thing on the telly,' he said to Molly, 'they have a computer and a dozen lovely girls at telephones to work with. And we can't even pick the right day. If we'd done this yesterday, we'd have heard the Hampden Roar. Ring, Ronnie, ring!'

'Calm down,' Molly said.

They waited. Without even the sound of numbers to pass the time, the minutes seemed endless. There was nothing to say. Keith divorced his mind from the waiting and tried to prepare a workable plan for the next morning. He jumped when the phone buzzed.

Ronnie sounded cheerful. 'The first box I tried was vandalised,' he said, 'and there was a wifie in the other one. Well, there's a band here all right, playing one of yon rumty-tumty marches.'

'We know,' Keith said. 'And Inspector Cathcart's on his way to join you, and so's the van. Keep your eyes open for Danny Bruce while we talk.'

'You'll be lucky,' Ronnie said. 'Fat chance! Sunday lunchtime in Glasgow and the day as dreary as a cow's bum. There's hardly a soul . . .' Silence fell. Just as Keith was wondering whether the connection had been broken, Ronnie's voice came back. 'You jammy bugger!' he said. 'There he goes, by God! Just as you said, even to the wee pluke beside his mouth.'

'Don't let him see you staring at him.' Keith heard his own voice crack. Molly and Jake were gaping at him.

'He's facing away,' Ronnie said, 'and I'm watching out o' the corner of my eye . . . He's crossing the street to the corner of Royal Crescent. He's stopped, as if he's waiting for somebody, but he's having a damn good keek around.' There was a pause which Keith used to relay the gist of the situation to the others. 'He's moving again,' Ronnie said. 'Round the Crescent. Stopped again. I canna' see him for a parked van, but I ken fine he's there.' Another hiatus. 'Aye. There he goes. I didna' see the number, but it's the only bright blue door.'

'He went in?'

'A camel coat did.'

'Good enough. Give me the number of the box and then hang up so that the others can get through. Wait in the box.'

'I can't do that,' Ronnie said. 'There's a mannie wanting in now. It may be urgent. I'm going to see if I can spot the right flat.'

'Don't do that,' Keith roared, but Ronnie had hung up.

'It's been a guddle, a proper pig's breakfast, from beginning to end,' Keith said. He was sitting with his head in his hands. 'Now that we've almost done it, that stupid sod's going in on his own. He saw Danny Bruce going into a stair in Royal Crescent. At least, he said it was Danny Bruce. Knowing Ronnie, he's probably just about to burst into the Lord Provost's love-nest. Get back into the other room, Janet. If Ronnie hasn't fouled it up, Danny Bruce should be calling about now.'

'I'm sure Ronnie'll do his best,' Molly said shakily.

'That's what I'm afraid of.'

'So am I.'

The phone rang in the sanctum and Danny Bruce's voice came over the speakers. Pop music was playing in the background. 'That's why he hung up so quickly,' Jake said. 'He wanted to cut off the noise of the band, and now he's got a radio playing.'

'Is your phone secure now?' Danny Bruce was saying.

'Yes.'

'Let's get on with it then. Turn that thing down slightly,' Bruce's voice added.

'I *beg* your pardon,' said Janet.

'Not you, my dear.' Danny Bruce sounded abashed.

'He's got somebody with him,' Keith said despairingly. 'He met some henchman on the doorstep and Ronnie didn't even notice.' The secretary's phone buzzed and Keith grabbed it up. 'Yes?'

It was Inspector Cathcart. 'I'm at Queen's Park,' he said. 'Sorry to have been so long. I thought it'd be quicker to use a public phone than to try for a link through the car's radio, but the first phone I tried had been vandalised, and in this one there was a rough-looking character who told me to push off.'

'You arrested him?' Keith said hopefully.

'No, why?'

Keith tried to think what he would do to Ronnie, but his mind was preoccupied. He would give the matter his attention later. 'I'm afraid that was my brother-in-law,' he said. 'He saw Danny Bruce go in through the bright blue door in Royal Crescent and he's followed him. Can you get over there, sharpish?'

'On my way.' The phone went dead.

Danny Bruce had resumed the reading of numbers but he broke off again. He must have turned away from the telephone, for his voice was barely audible over the background music. 'Somebody on the landing,' he said. 'See that they don't linger.'

'*Oh my God!*' Molly said. '*Ronnie's going to be killed!*'

Janet said later that the next few seconds were filled with noises that might have made a sound-track for the climax of some radio melodrama after the 'Dick Barton' school – fists and grunts and voices shouting – except that instead of the 'Ride of the Valkyries' Danny Bruce's radio was playing a minuet. Then somebody lurched against a table, the telephone went down and they were left with the dialling-tone coming faithfully over the speakers.

Molly's face was white, and her eyes looked large and black. Keith judged that she was close to hysteria. Any distraction, even if it angered her, would be the better for her. 'Janet,' he said, 'there's nothing more we can do for the moment. Be a love and pop out for fish suppers all round and something to drink.'

Molly rounded on him. 'Keith Calder! How can you talk about food? Ronnie may be being killed.'

'I told him not to go in there.'

'And when I say Ronnie's being killed, *don't smile!*'

'Sorry,' Keith said. 'It's subconscious.'

That did it. The insult to her brother kept Molly on the boil for the next few minutes. Her tirade was still in flood when the phone buzzed for the last time and Inspector Cathcart spoke to Keith.

'We got him,' Cathcart said. 'And the money. And now you'd better be able to put your mouth where the money is and prove where it came from.'

Molly dragged the phone out of her husband's grasp. 'Is Ronnie all right?'

'Is that Mrs Calder? Yes, your brother's fine, just a bit above himself. He took it on himself to administer the caution, and he got it wrong.'

Keith was listening, his ear beside Molly's. 'That's Ronnie he's talking about, all right,' he said.

'Stay where you are,' Cathcart said. 'I'll be with you as soon as I can.'

During the two hours and more that intervened before Inspector Cathcart's arrival Keith went into a trance and paced about the room, leaving it to Molly to help the others restore Mr Enterkin's rooms and gather up Jake's tools and gear. When Molly sent Janet to help Jake carry his things back to the shop and told her not to hurry back, Keith came out of his brown study to suggest that if and when she returned she might bring some food with her, and he was then lost to the world again. Grumbling, Molly opened her purse.

When Janet did come back, too soon for Molly's liking, she brought beer with her, and parcels of fish and chips, and they sat down at Enterkin's desk to eat and enjoy a meal that would have offended that gourmet's sensibilities.

Later, Keith began to talk. As far as he was concerned the reward for the money was already as good as in the bank, and he had already put it out of his mind. The gems which had been in the second pistol, he thought, were beyond their recovery and he wasted no time on them. Logic suggested that Noddy's corpse might already be in Glasgow, but quite apart from Cathcart's information Keith had a gut-hunch to the contrary. And Keith believed that hunches were no more than logic not yet recognised by the conscious mind.

Starting from the known facts Keith, who knew the surrounding countryside rather better than the back of his hand, started building theories to explain the missing links in the chain of facts. He invited the girls to knock his theories down and then exploded them himself. He paced about the room. He phoned Mr Ledbetter at home and learned that the red hire-car was being collected from a Glasgow car-park but that the white car had reappeared on the garage forecourt during the previous night. Fretting over these new facts, Keith devised more theories, but each one had a damning flaw.

'There's something I haven't thought of,' he said at

last. 'And it's so close! It's as if I once had it in my mind but let it go ...'

Molly had seen Keith in these moods before. 'Never mind,' she said. 'Take your mind off it and it'll come back to you. Anyway, we got half of what we set out for. And that's above par for the course, so you've done well.'

'More than that,' Janet said. 'He ... I thought it was a brilliant performance.'

Molly looked at her coldly. When she married Keith, Molly had known what she was taking on. She had too much sense to show jealousy, which might have been the one thing that could shake Keith's new-found faith in marriage and in his own ability to stay faithful. But, on the other hand, she had no intention of encouraging other girls to hang around Keith, admiring the charm which he exuded so easily and responding to it in a way that just might strike a response in him.

'What happens next?' Molly asked briskly.

Keith withdrew his speculative look from Janet. 'I think,' he said to Molly, 'that we've got to accept that whatever was in the second pistol is beyond our grasp. But poor Noddy's corpse is probably still around. With all that police activity I doubt if they could have got it out last night, and it isn't a job to be done by daylight. But by now they've had a chance to get organised.'

'Organised what way?' Molly asked nervously.

'Cathcart may be able to give us a hint. He says they've been looking up contacts in the car trade. If Spence and Curran have already left Glasgow then it's odds-on they've got a map and a Land Rover. They'd probably come over the moors by daylight until they can see the town, and then come down after dark.'

'And if they're still in Glasgow?'

'Then they're probably coming in by road and taking him out up past Gerry's cottage.'

Janet, irritated at having lost Keith's attention, was twisting in her chair and showing an escalating length of pretty leg; but by force of will Molly held Keith's eyes. 'We've got a reward coming,' she said. 'Can't we take it and opt out? If it isn't enough to buy Briesland House, then I shan't mind.'

'I don't like being beaten,' Keith said rebelliously.

He looked very young when he spoke like that and turned his head that way, Molly thought – like a small boy trying to evade a bath. She tried not to sound maternal. 'And I don't want you to be beaten. But, Keith, those two men are bad news. According to you, they're coming to collect a dead body, and they've already killed another man for it, so why would a few more deaths matter to them? You want to lurk in the dark and wait for them to come, and when they've got what they came for, you think you can jump out and take it away from them. Right?'

Keith flushed. 'You're over-simplifying,' he said.

'I'm not, and you know it. Well, if you're proposing to take stupid chances with your life, and Ronnie's, just to get me Briesland House then I don't want the bloody place. Or is it that you've taken a scunner to those two? Do you want revenge because they made you look silly?' She wanted to ask if he wasn't just playing at cops and robbers.

'Believe me,' Keith said, 'I've no intention of taking chances. But you've been very patient while we built up the business, and now I want to give you what you've been waiting for, a proper home of your own, heated and furnished and carpeted the way you'd like it. I want to do this for you, and you can't expect me to stop now that we're half-way.'

Molly sighed. 'Think, then,' she said. 'Think hard and bust the problem before they get here.'

'That's what I'm trying to do,' Keith said pettishly, 'but you two keep blethering.' He relapsed into silent thought.

Janet pursed her lips and went to stare out of the window against the sun. Molly nodded to herself.

FOURTEEN

When the knocking came at the door below, Keith went down to answer it. He opened the door and stepped back quickly.

'I'm Cathcart,' said the stranger. 'So help me it's cold over this side of the hills. You're expecting trouble?' he asked, with a nod at Keith's gun.

'Just being careful,' Keith said. 'Come away in. You're here before the others.'

'I passed them before Galashiels,' Cathcart said as they started to climb. 'Well, now, which would you expect to get here first, your pal Hay in a Daimler near as old as himself, or me driving a police Jag. with everything flashing?'

'You,' Keith said, 'definitely. So we needn't expect them yet a while.'

In Mr Enterkin's office, Keith introduced Inspector Cathcart to the two girls. Cathcart was younger than Keith had expected, taller, heavier, round-faced and fair-haired – as different as he could be, in fact, from Keith's mental picture of him. The telephone, with all its distortions, had been unfair to Cathcart. Keith had disliked him over the phone, and had trusted him only because no alternative was available; but he liked the inspector on first sight, and knew that his trust would not be betrayed.

It seemed natural that Cathcart should take Mr Enterkin's swivel-chair and that Keith should fetch another chair for himself. The inspector's bulk and forcefulness relegated Keith to second place. 'I didn't think you could

194

pull it off,' he said when they were settled. 'In fact, you'll never know how nearly I told you to hand over what you'd got and leave it to the experts. But then I remembered how often we'd tried and got nowhere, and I thought that a new approach might pay off. And it did. But if you ever come up with a chance like that again, don't jump the gate. Or I suppose you'd say "Go off at half-cock".'

'No, I wouldn't,' Keith said.

'Well, I would,' Cathcart said, smiling. 'You succeeded, but you could have blown it badly because you didn't have a tenth of the resources that the job needed. Given a little time we could have set up for call-tracing, we could have had radio communications, cars, shadows, the lot.'

'And,' Keith said, 'you could have blown it by being too active and making Danny Bruce suspicious.'

'That I don't deny,' Cathcart said fairly. 'You'd better tell me the whole story.'

Between them they led the inspector through the whole tale. He was a good audience. He laughed himself out of breath at Keith's misadventures in the wash-house and shook his head over Munro's refusal to believe in the demise of Noddy Chalmers. He listened intently to the salient parts of the tapes.

'There you are,' he said at last. 'You had the devil's own luck. Ambulance, model aircraft and a brass band. Three of the most penetrating noises you could expect!'

'If it hadn't been one thing it might have been another,' Keith said. 'We had to go straight ahead and act. Now that Munro has a proven murder on his hands, he'll be wanting complete statements.'

'That may have been a good reason as far as you were concerned, but it was a bad one from the standpoint of justice,' Cathcart said. 'You accepted a reduced chance of success in order to increase your own chance of a reward.'

'But we succeeded,' Molly reminded him.

'The fact remains. And,' Cathcart said, 'if I don't clock in with the local force before they notice my Jag. in their car-park, the fat'll be in the fire. But I'd like to get your statements down first. What you might call a debriefing.'

'You're not debriefing me on our first date,' Janet said. She fluttered her eyelashes at him.

The taking of statements was interrupted by the arrival of Hamish, who was his usual quiet self, and Ronnie, who had swung from caustic disbelief to triumphant assurance and a blind faith that Keith could be expected to pull more rabbits out of hats at any moment. Sir Peter had dropped the pair and had departed for home and urgent business, but sent messages of congratulation and a promise to visit and confer shortly.

Patience is a characteristic of a good policeman. Cathcart waited and smiled, like an uncle at a children's party, while the five compared notes, exchanged felicitations and criticism, did calculations as to the probable value of their shares in the reward and speculated as to just where the *hell* Noddy Chalmers could be.

In the babble, only Molly heard the phone ringing in the outer office. She went to answer it and came back. 'It's your sergeant,' she told Cathcart.

Cathcart rejoined them in a few minutes. 'Danny Bruce has hardly said a word,' he told them. 'But he sent a message. He wants to know if Cynthia would like to marry an ageing widower. He thinks they'd make a great team.'

'Do you think I should?' Janet asked.

'Tell him that he'll have to wait for her to grow up,' Ronnie said. Janet blew a raspberry.

'And he didn't want to say anything about his daughter, but there's no doubt that he's worried,' Cathcart said. 'But the real point of the message was to say that Curran and Spence have just left Glasgow, going east, in a breakdown truck.'

'Then all you have to do,' Molly said, 'is what you ought to have done all along. Get Inspector Munro to put men to watch them and they'll lead him to Noddy. With Mr Cathcart here as a witness – '

Keith jerked upright in his chair. 'By St Christopher's holy fart! ' he said loudly.

Talk stopped dead.

'*What* did you say?' Molly asked sternly.

Keith ignored her. 'I've got it,' he said. 'I've bloody *got* it. We don't have to follow anybody. I know where Noddy is.'

'I tell you it's obvious,' Keith said. 'What the hell do you think they'd want a breakdown vehicle for?'

'Transport?' Ronnie suggested vaguely.

'Do you suppose,' Molly said, 'that Noddy's in the boot of a car that's broken down?'

Keith shook his head. 'You'll have to do better than that. They'd just swap him into another car. Anyway, there isn't a vehicle that's not accounted for. No, it's simpler than that and more obvious. They want to use the crane.'

'Crane?'

'They want,' Keith said patiently, 'to lift something heavy.'

'Like what?' asked Janet.

'Like Noddy.'

'Noddy isn't heavy,' Molly objected. 'Not what you'd call heavy. Not heavy enough to need a crane.'

'He is now,' Keith said. 'Something's been happening that's made him very heavy indeed. Let me give you another theory, what they call a scenario, and you can see if you can spot any holes in it.

'Two nights ago, we caught the two men up by Gerry's cottage. Remember? Well, this is what I think happened. They humped the body up there, intending to fetch a car up to the main road and spirit it away. But only when they got to the cottage did they realise that the hillside below the main road is as near as dammit a cliff. No way could anyone climb it unassisted, with a body on his back. So they hid the body and went to collect some rope. They stole Harry Glynn's car and Spence, being the stronger man, took the rope and drove Harry's car up to the top. Curran walked up again, to attach the body to the rope. But we turned up and chased Spence into the hills, and Ronnie put a couple of shots close past Curran and then sat tight with a rifle. Even if Ronnie hadn't been there, I doubt if they had a rendez-vous nearer than Glasgow. So I think they came back last night with a decent bit of rope. And that's when they found out what had happened.'

Janet turned round from the window. 'Well, what *had* happened?' she asked.

'Ronnie,' said Keith. 'If you were at the gable of Gerry's cottage with a corpse to hide, where would be the best place to put it?'

Ronnie looked baffled. Hamish said 'Water-barrel.'

'Exactly,' Keith said. 'I think they'd stowed Noddy in the water-barrel. Only, remember, one hell of a record-breaking frost was just starting. The canal's frozen inches thick by now, so just imagine a water-barrel with the cold air getting all around it. Noddy was frozen into a solid barrel of ice. It must weigh a ton or more. You don't haul that up a cliff on a bit of clothes-line.'

Cathcart pointed a finger at Keith. 'So instead of waiting for the thaw and risking somebody else getting there first, they're coming over with the breakdown truck to haul the whole caboodle up the cliff and drive it away to Glasgow?'

'You've got it,' Keith said. 'Now, can anybody think of any other reason why they might want a breakdown vehicle?'

They looked at each other in silence. 'That has to be the answer,' Cathcart said.

'God!' said Hamish. 'If it weren't so macabre it'd be damned funny. I wish Molly'd been hidden there with her camera to take their faces when they looked into the barrel.'

'Well,' Keith said, 'she wasn't. And she won't be there tonight either.'

'I don't think any of us should be there,' Molly said. 'I think it's the job of the police from now on. After all, you could hardly lose out on the reward now.'

Ronnie, Hamish and Keith swapped sidelong glances. A woman would never sympathise with a man's urge to follow up and be in at the kill.

'I expect that Inspector Cathcart agrees with you,' Keith said. 'And if Noddy's in the water-barrel Munro could certainly collect him. But I don't see Munro handling the arrest of two armed men like those. I think he'd blow it. Well, I suppose it's no skin off our noses.'

'It's skin off mine,' Cathcart said. 'Oh, I agree with Mrs Calder. It's Munro's job. But Archie Curran killed a mate of mine.' Cathcart's voice was so cold that Keith gave an involuntary shiver. He hoped that nobody ever spoke about him like that. 'He killed him quite deliberately and in cold blood,' Cathcart went on, 'but we couldn't prove it and I can't arrest him for it. But – oh God! – how I want the satisfaction of taking him in for this and telling him that what it's really all about is Billy Duffus!'

'You'll be needing some help,' Keith said.

'I don't want Munro's help, even if I have to hand Curran over to him ten seconds after I make the pinch. But I could do with a few of Munro's men. Let me play this by ear and see what I can win out of it. You listen carefully and be prepared to bear witness that I've told nothing but the absolute literal truth. What's the number of the local nick?'

'I'll get it for you,' Keith said.

Molly was an experienced judge of a man's line of patter. Once he had Munro on the line, Cathcart showed a talent for what Mr Enterkin would have called *suggestio falsi* and *suppressio veri* which she thought came close to rivalling Keith's, and he had much the same wicked glint in his eye.

' . . . Chief Inspector Munro? Inspector Cathcart, Strathclyde. Yes, we've met. Now, I know fine you're busy with a killing on your hands, so I'll be brief. We've just made a recovery, in Glasgow, of a large part of the money embezzled by John Galloway, who belongs in your parts. I may say that this was thanks to your Mr Keith Calder, whom I think you know. I'm back in Newton Lauder with him now . . . Yes, I'll see that he comes in for a chat when I've finished with him. Is that all right?'

Munro's voice came quacking out of the receiver like a remote, Hebridean duck. Cathcart covered the mouthpiece. 'True so far?'

'Masterly,' Keith said.

'That's fine,' Cathcart said into the phone. 'I just

didn't want to be on your patch without letting you know. And there are one or two other things. I've had a tip that a couple of villains are headed in this direction. They're driving a breakdown truck, and one of them is armed. They probably won't come into Newton Lauder, but just in case they do I suggest that you tell your road-blocks that they're to be let through, reported over the radio, and then followed at a distance. I'll be in touch from time to time.'

Munro spoke again. Cathcart raised his eyebrows at Keith. 'Nothing but the truth, right?' he said.

'Right,' said Keith.

'Finally, about Mr Calder again,' Cathcart said. 'He's got some bee in his bonnet about another body that he says he's already told you about. He says that it's to do with this case of mine and that he's finally worked out where the body's got to be. He's got some story about it being the body of some sort of courier who brought a whole lot of stolen jewels through for John Galloway to buy with the embezzled money and take abroad with him . . . Yes, it does sound a bit like a bad play on the telly, doesn't it? But I'll get no sense out of the man unless I let him go and look there. Is it all right with you if I go a bit out of the town with him and take a look? If you've any doubts, you might send a couple of constables along with us.'

Munro's voice squawked softly. Cathcart hung up. He looked rueful. 'I laid it on too thick,' he said. 'I could have done with a couple of Munro's men along. But, "Anything that Mr Calder tells you, you can take with a whole cart-load of salt," he says. "Go body-hunting with him, and my best wishes".'

Keith found that Ronnie and Hamish were looking at him expectantly. 'Probably just as well,' he said. 'A brace of unarmed bobbies might be useful eyes and ears, but I wouldn't see them being much help against Curran's pistol backed by the man-mountain. If I took a pistol out of stock, would you be authorised to carry it?'

'No,' said Cathcart. 'And my head really would be in a sling if I carried one without authorisation. But I've taken a gun off an armed man before, *and* used it on his mate.'

Keith looked at the other's stubborn jaw. He thought that Cathcart and Ronnie would make a fine pair of matched book-ends. 'And policemen have been killed trying it,' he said. 'Well, we can't help you out. We've got a date for a pigeon-shoot up by Gerry Reynolds' cottage.'

Cathcart's jaw looked a little less stubborn, and there was even the trace of a smile around his eyes. 'It's against the law to shoot on the Sabbath,' he said.

'Not people it isn't,' Ronnie said. 'The Act doesn't say anything about people.'

Keith had been expecting Molly to protest against the idea of any further physical action, but she regarded the presence of a policeman as a talisman against all harm. 'Just as long as you stay with the inspector and do whatever he tells you,' she said.

Inspector Cathcart was less used to walking rough country than were the others, and he was still puffing unhappily when Keith overtook them at the top of the track. Keith had eased his own mind by asking each of the girls, in private, to look after the other, and then settling them in the flat with instructions to lock and bolt the doors and to open up for no voice that they could not recognise.

'You didn't have to gallop up here like mountain goats,'

Cathcart was grumbling. 'They can't be here yet, and if the warm front brings fog they could be hours yet.'

'You needed the exercise,' Ronnie said.

They peered out from the concealment of the twin hedges. 'There could be an advance-guard,' Keith said, 'but if there is it's not here yet.'

The sun was behind the hills and the cottage stood, bleak and lonely, in the deep shadow that lay over that side of the valley. Already a brilliant moon sailed high in the south. Cautiously, the four men came into the open and approached the water-barrel. Ronnie put down his ancient hammer-gun and lifted off the heavy cover.

Cathcart polished the surface of the ice with his sleeve and used his pocket-torch. He gave a quick shiver which might have been from the cold. 'You're right once again,' he said. 'There's somebody in here. I couldn't swear that it was Noddy Chalmers, but I can see one foot and part of another.' He stepped back.

Ronnie put the cover back in place. 'Could we not roll it down the hill?' he asked. 'That'd get Noddy beyond the reach of those two.'

'We could,' Keith said. 'But we couldn't control it, not at that weight. It'd take off down the hill, all the way to the cop-shop across the square.'

'That's where it'd be taken anyway,' Ronnie persisted. 'Would it make it up the steps, d'you think? Maybe all the way to Munro's office?'

'My car's in the way,' Keith said.

'What did you bring that wee thing for?'

'To catch you beggars up before you did something silly, like rolling that barrel down the hill.'

'We're not moving that barrel an inch,' Cathcart said firmly. 'I want to catch them in the act. Otherwise, their presence here doesn't mean a thing. But catch them trying to remove the barrel and you link them with the other crimes.' He looked up at the edge of the road above. They could hear the sound of a lone car, climbing the long slope of the main road. 'Which way will they come?'

'Down the hill from your right,' Hamish said.

'They'll stop up there. One man climbs down by rope, attaches the wire and up she goes. Right?'

'Right,' said Keith.

'Then,' Cathcart said, 'I think we want somebody at the top. Just as a precaution.'

'You, Hamish,' Keith said. 'You do the most climbing.'

'Aye. But I'll need something to sling my gun.'

'I'll see what I can find,' Keith said. He left the others and let himself into Gerry Reynolds' cottage. There was nothing of use in the kitchen, but in the living-room he picked up a ball of string. Having penetrated so far, he thought that he might just as well check the rest of the cottage, and in Gerry's bedroom he saw something that interested him very much indeed. He nodded to it and left the cottage, locking up and dropping the key into his pocket. He paused for a moment on the doorstep and looked over the town. A slow grin split his face. Then, wiping his face clear of any trace of a smile, he walked round the corner of the cottage to join the others.

While Hamish fashioned himself a sling, Cathcart spoke. 'You get across the road and into hiding,' he told Hamish. 'If you seem to be needed, come out fast. Otherwise, stay put. And don't forget that your first job's to disable the vehicle; they'll be lost without transport. You,' he told Ronnie, 'will be in the bushes over the far side. Mr Calder and I will stay by the cottage. When they come, we'll wait until there's no disputing what they came for. Then I'll go out and tell them that they're under arrest. If and when they resist and only then, you three can come out of hiding.'

Hamish whistled softly. 'You're a braver man than I am,' he said.

'Very likely,' said Ronnie.

'What if Curran pulls out his pop-gun,' Keith said, 'and looks like shooting you?'

'In that eventuality, don't hang about.'

'Got you,' said Keith. 'It'll be a pleasure.'

Hamish started up the wall of rock as effortlessly as a spider going up its web.

'Like an ape, isn't he?' Ronnie said.

'Stay down there, ground-hog,' came Hamish's voice from above, 'and I'll pelt you with coconuts.' Then he was over the top and out of sight.

Keith looked at his watch. 'I think I'll take a good look inside the cottage,' he said. 'Just in case. And I might do a wee patrol.'

Cathcart nodded. 'If a vehicle stops, or if you hear voices, come back fast and quietly.'

Keith unlocked the cottage door and went back inside.

The interior of the cottage seemed hot after the chill outside. Keith put down his gun in the hall and took off his heavy anorak. Then he went through into the bedroom.

'Good evening,' he said.

By the light of the lamp which Gerry Reynolds had left burning to deter intruders, supplemented by the last daylight filtering through the curtains, Keith studied his find. Dourly, over the silk scarf that was tied tightly round her face, Mary Bruce stared back at him. Keith walked round her once. Her wrists had been tied behind her with nylon climbing-rope, and her ankles bound. It had been done by a skilled hand, for there was no escaping and yet the blood was not cut off from her fingers. Thereafter, she had been sat in Gerry's sturdy bedside chair and roped firmly to that.

Keith untied and removed the silk scarf and pulled out the sodden handkerchief that was gagging her. From the initials, both belonged to the absent owner of the cottage. Keith sat down facing her, on Gerry's bed.

Mary Bruce worked her jaw and lips. Her makeup was smeared and the corners of her mouth were reddened, but she was still, Keith thought, a very attractive woman. His description of her to Molly had been tempered in the direction of what a wife prefers to hear. 'Thank God,' she said hoarsely. 'I thought you mightn't be coming back.'

'Did you think I'd leave an old friend to starve?'

'Worse. I thought you might be going to leave this old friend until those . . .' She stopped.

'Frank Hutch's boys?'

'You know that, do you?' She shivered once, as if with fear or pleasure. It came back into Keith's mind that as a business contact she had been firm and ruthless, but that as soon as the occasion became social her sexuality had expressed itself in a feminine subservience which, like Janet's, had been an open invitation to domination or even cruelty. Keith was adept at reading a woman's mind, and he began to have certain thoughts about Mary Bruce.

'We know,' Keith said. 'We know an awful lot. I think we've just about got the whole story.' He watched her carefully, trying to interpret her tiniest shifts of expression.

'Aren't you going to untie me?' she asked.

Keith lay back on the quilt. 'How long have you been there?'

'Too damn long. Since about three this morning.'

206

'Then a little longer won't hurt you. What do you want first, the good news or the bad news?'

She tried to shrug, then threw up her eyes. 'Now he wants to play games! If there's any more bad news to come you'd better break it to me now.'

'All right, brace yourself. The Strathclyde fuzz just picked up your dad in possession of most of the money that John Galloway embezzled. They know that it was paid over for the jewels from the Prestwick robbery. They've found Noddy's little corpse with half the jewels in him, and they know that he worked for Danny. There's a hell of a good case building up against him for resetting.'

For ten seconds she hung her head. Then she stiffened. 'Get me out of these damn ropes, you bastard,' she said. 'There's things I've got to do.'

'Not if you call me names,' Keith said.

She slumped again, and Keith waited. 'He was careful, but it was bound to happen some time,' she said at last. Keith saw that there were tears on her cheeks. 'Wipe my face,' she said.

Keith sat up. He took out his handkerchief and gently wiped her face dry. 'Don't you want the good news?' he asked.

'What is it?'

'You can buy your way out of this mess.'

'I'm not in it,' she said indignantly.

'You came through here,' Keith said patiently, 'as soon as the jewels and the money went adrift. You brought a hired gun who got himself killed. You flitted around the place in a blonde wig and dark glasses, during which time half of the hot gems went missing from your dad's courier's motor-bike. You're in it, my girl, right up to the ears I used to nibble. But you're in a great position to buy yourself out.'

'How?'

'You can put the finger on Archie Curran. I'm surprised he left you alive.'

'So was I,' she said and shivered again.

'There's an inspector here from Glasgow. Curran killed his mate. If you could shop Curran for killing Wallace, I think I could get him to promise you immunity. You did see Curran do the deed?'

She nodded. 'He hit Peter – Peter Wallace – from behind with a pipe from one of those water-trough things. But I was in the bushes and he didn't know I'd seen him. When they caught me watching them last night I pretended that I still wanted to know what had happened to Peter. I think maybe that saved my life. Curran made out that he'd scared Peter away. He said that he was leaving me alive for the moment in case he found that he wanted a hold over Dad, but that if he didn't he'd leave me in the water-butt when he came back for wee Noddy.'

'Did they search you?' Keith said suddenly.

She hesitated for a second too long. And then she nodded. 'Beasts,' she said. But it was a lie. Keith was sure that Archie Curran had never known of the existence of a second pistol.

'Will you testify against Curran?' Keith asked.

She stared at him whitely and bit her lip. 'Nobody, but nobody, clypes on Archie Curran without something awful happening to them.'

Keith sighed. 'But something awful, like prison, is going to happen to you if you don't. Think about it. Your father's going up the river for a few years. Well, with his money and connections I dare say he can arrange to pass the time without too much misery. But don't tell me that he doesn't have money salted away abroad where you can get at it. The shops could run themselves for a while, and the other business is finished for now anyway. And if Curran goes down, you've nothing to worry about for years.'

'I'd rather just beat it out of here now,' she said.

'Go on, then.'

She pulled against the ropes. 'Untie me, you sod,' she snapped.

'Not yet. We're laying a trap for Archie Curran. You could say that we're doing you a favour. You can wait and think about it for that long.'

'I'm bloody uncomfortable,' she said coaxingly. 'Untie me, Keith. Just for a few minutes.'

Keith nearly laughed. 'Not just yet a while,' he said. 'You're too slippery by half. I don't see myself getting your hands tied again without losing some skin, and I've been dunted on the head once already in the last few days. You stay as you are and I'll see if I can't make you a bit more comfortable.' He got up and walked round her. 'Your bra's hurting you, isn't it?'

She fought the ropes, Keith thought, like a trapped mink. 'No, it isn't,' she said between her teeth. 'You leave me alone, Keith Calder, or I'll have you up for indecent assault.'

Keith slid down the zip at the back of her dress and unhooked her bra. She tried to beat him off by striking backwards at his chest with her head, but he slipped his hands down her front and round her generous breasts. 'I thought so,' he said. 'You looked just a little bit too smug when I said that we knew the whole story.' He brought out two packages that crunched when he fingered them.

'Keith, *please*,' she wailed. 'I'll give you half. That's better than you'll get from the insurers.'

'They're not yours to give, sweetheart,' he said. He weighed the warm packages in his hands before slipping them into his pockets. 'I'll just have to make do with ten per cent. I envy those stones, but they can't have been comfortable for you.'

She managed a small laugh. 'For that money, I could have stood the pain a little longer.'

'Look on the bright side. You don't have to stand the pain any longer. Shall I kiss the place and make it well?' Keith thought that, with her clothes in disarray and her hair flying, she looked . . . irresistible. He put his hands down and weighed her heavy breasts in his hands. They were beautifully shaped, soft and as exciting as lips.

She squirmed as much as she could. 'Leave me alone,' she said in a very small voice.

'You never used to say that.'

'You never had me tied up before.'

'If you were free, would you really fight me off?'

Mary gave no answer except to stop struggling and lean back against him. Quick shudders ran through her.

'This is more like old times,' Keith said.

He could feel her laughter. 'You always could get more out of me than I meant to give you,' she said. 'They were good times.'

'We went well together.'

She sighed under his hands. 'We never should have split up,' she said. 'It was when you stopped doing business with Dad, wasn't it? You were just a wee bit priggy and holier-than-thou. Dad didn't like that. He thought that you might be a danger, but I said that you might not want to play his games but you'd never grass, and anyway, I said I never talk in my sleep.'

'Doesn't he mind?'

'Me having a lover occasionally? No. He knows I'm as careful as he is, and it makes him feel better about his fancy women. But then you didn't come round any more. I thought perhaps you were afraid that Dad was using me to persuade you round.'

'Perhaps.'

She twisted her head to look at him. 'That's one thing I wouldn't do.'

'Accept my apologies.'

'This is hellish uncomfortable,' she said, moving uneasily. 'Let me stand up for a minute or two.'

'I'm not letting you loose,' Keith said. 'I'll let you up for a minute if you want, but that's all. You've got too many tricks.'

'That's almost a compliment,' she said.

Keith unwound the many turns of climbing-rope and pulled her up. With her ankles still tied she swayed against him for balance. 'That's a bit better,' she said. 'But my bum has gone to sleep and now I've got pins and needles.'

'A rub might help,' Keith said. He rubbed. 'Just for old times' sake, of course.'

'Yes, of course. I hate to spoil the mood but I'll need to pay a little visit in a minute. You'll have to untie my hands.'

'What can you do for yourself,' Keith asked, 'that I can't do for you? And that I haven't done before?'

But later, as they lay on Gerry Reynolds' bed, Keith said, 'I'll untie your hands if you like.'

'Don't be a fool,' she said. 'This is the most exciting thing that ever happened to me . . . Keith, if I give evidence and then go out to a place Dad's got near Benidorm, would you come and see me sometimes?'

Keith stilled his movement for a few seconds. 'I'm a married man now,' he said stiffly.

FIFTEEN

When Keith came yawning out of the cottage, the sun was quite gone and the moon was brilliant over the frosted scene. He held his face up to the cold air to drive away sleep before moving round the corner of the cottage. There was black shadow under the cliff, but the gable was almost floodlit. Ronnie and Cathcart were chatting softly, squatting in the shadow of the water-barrel.

Keith crouched beside them. 'You should be over in the bushes,' he told Ronnie.

'When I'm good and ready,' Ronnie said. 'If you're so worried you go over there. How come you've been so long?'

Keith spoke to Cathcart. 'I've been doing some more investigating,' he said, 'and I've got a witness who saw Archie Curran kill the Englishman, Wallace.'

Ronnie gave a low whistle. 'What did you do? Wave your magic wand again?'

'Something very like that.' Keith smiled secretly in the shadow. 'The point is, this witness will only testify in exchange for immunity in respect of a minor part in the fencing of the jewels. Can you swing that?'

Cathcart hesitated. 'I'm not allowed to make promises in the name of the Procurator Fiscal,' he began.

'Who's this witness?' Ronnie asked.

'Never you mind just now,' Keith said. 'Inspector, shouldn't we be getting into position?'

'We needn't hurry,' Cathcart said. 'It could be a long wait. They'll probably stop for a meal and time themselves to get here after the traffic's died away. And we're not too badly placed as we are. We can scatter in a second or two if we hear their truck pull up.'

'All right. Molly appointed you our nanny,' Keith said. 'So what about the immunity question?'

'It's tricky,' Cathcart said. 'Wallace's murder took place over here. But the theft of the jewels was in Strathclyde, and the fence was arrested there, so any offences in connection with those same things would almost certainly be tried in Glasgow. I won't know for sure until I've spoken to both Fiscals, but I could promise your witness a ninety per cent. chance of immunity. You're sure he can bring Curran down?'

'I don't think there's any doubt about it,' Keith said. He slanted his watch to the light of the moon. 'Ronnie, I think you'd better be moving over the other side.'

'And I think he'd better not,' said a high and fluting voice, and Archie Curran came round the front corner of the cottage. He was carrying a shotgun, sawn off at barrels and stock, and Keith thought that even the worst shot in the world could hardly miss with such a weapon at ten feet range.

Hughie Spence came round the other corner.

'Put your guns on the ground and stand up.'

Ronnie had already laid down his gun while he chatted to Cathcart. Keith's gun, a Winchester Super X, was under his wrong arm and Cathcart was in the way. With a sick sense of doom, Keith lowered the weapon. Even in such an emergency it was too expensive a gun to throw down. He leaned it carefully against the wall and stood away.

When he had the three men backed against the cottage wall, Curran gave a mirthless snort of laughter. He switched the sawn-off gun to his left hand and from under his coat he pulled out the silenced automatic. 'If you feel like trying something, go right ahead,' he said. 'I'd rather not make loud bangs just yet, but if I miss with this – ' he hefted the automatic ' – I'll blow you apart with the other one and we'll be gone long before the police get here, if they bother to come at all to investigate a shot or two on the hill. And if somebody stops their car to see what all the noise is about, it'll be too bad about them as well. So, if anyone prefers to die sooner than later, and slowly rather than quickly, who am I to say them nay? Hughie?'

'Yes, Boss?' The hoarse whisper was almost drowned by the rumble of a heavy vehicle climbing the hill overhead.

Curran waited until the rumble died uncaringly away. 'Calder was talking about a witness. He must mean the girl. Go and see if she's still there. And if she is . . .'

'I'll fetch her out here?'

Curran paused and, suicide or not, Keith prepared himself for a running tackle. Then Curran shrugged. 'All right, bring her out. Time enough when we're sure that we don't need her any more.'

Hughie Spence nodded, and moved off with his curiously light step round the front of the cottage. They heard him try the door, grunt and put his shoulder to it. Wood splintered.

A vehicle coasted to a halt above them with no more sound than a faint groan of brakes. A door was gently closed and the driver's feet gritted on the road. A figure appeared against the stars.

'Let down your cable,' Curran said, 'and put your lamp on.' Seconds later a light shone down from the vehicle's roof, filling in the shadows and putting an end to Keith's hopes that a sudden cloud over the moon might give him a chance.

Cathcart cleared his throat. 'Don't be a fool to yourself, Curran,' he said. 'My colleagues know where I am, and they know that I've been keeping tabs on you all day. They told me the minute you left Glasgow. You might get away with what you've done so far, but you know how we react when one of our own gets chopped. They'll be after you with everything they've got within minutes.'

'Within minutes of putting the pieces back together and making sure it's you,' Curran said. Under the stark light of the moon, his face, with its inky shadows, belonged in the darkest corner of hell. 'And then they've got to catch me. And I'll be long gone.'

'Leaving Frank Hutch and the others to whistle for their shares in the jewels?'

Curran glanced up. As if in answer, the truck's starter whirred. 'Along with anyone else who thinks that they can cut themselves a piece,' Curran agreed. 'But you try to suggest that when they come back and I'll cut you in half before you can get three words out.'

Spence came back with the girl under one arm. He carried her as easily as a pillow, and as casually dropped her near Keith's feet. She was weeping through a fresh gag. 'She'd been moved to the bed,' the big man whispered, 'and her gag was out. She wanted to scream, so . . .'

'Somebody helped himself,' Curran said. 'I wonder what else he got out of her.'

'She didn't have anything to say,' Keith said quickly. The two packets of stones seemed to be grinding into his thighs. 'Can't I at least untie her now?'

'Leave her,' Curran said.

A cable came snaking down the cliff and the big man

dragged the end across the flat ground and round the barrel, shackling it back on itself. He waved, and they heard the drum of the crane start to turn. The cable moved, began to lift off the ground. The driver returned to watch from the cliff's edge. He was holding a submachine gun that looked to Keith like a wartime Beretta, and he seemed to be holding it with comfortable familiarity.

'For God's sake,' Cathcart said, 'it's going to fall on the girl.'

'I don't suppose it'll matter,' Curran said almost without interest. 'I was saving her up in case I wanted a bargaining counter against her old man, but we're past that point now. The only reason that any of you are still breathing is that there's no point making a lot of noise before we have to. There are occasions when it would be foolish to leave live witnesses around, and this is one of them.'

The cable tightened and the vehicle's exhaust became louder as the strain came on. The barrel groaned and shifted. Keith's growing fear for himself was swamped under the horror of waiting for the massive weight to topple onto the girl beneath.

The barrel moved an inch, and another. It moved in jerks and wobbles as the bricks beneath it shifted or rolled. Futile as the gesture would have been, Keith wanted to throw himself on top of the girl – to protect her from the irresistible weight, or to die, crushed into her in a final consummation. Then a brick slipped, the barrel groaned and hesitated and toppled sideways, away from the girl, to land with a crackling of timber and a thump that shook the frozen earth for an acre around.

Mary Bruce whimpered. Keith, seeing her body shake and feeling his own fear flood back, thought that the real horror of death was not death itself but the knowledge of its imminence and inevitability. This time, it was really going to happen. Well, he thought wryly, his last hour had been good, but he would rather have died with the memory of Molly in his loins.

Where the *hell* was Hamish?

The cable tautened again and the barrel began a slow, ponderous slither over the hard ground. Several of its staves projected like broken limbs. Curran and the big man stood facing the cottage wall and the three men ranged against it, just too far away to be rushed until the last, desperate moment when there would be nothing left to lose.

Hamish, for God's sake!

Or had Hamish already been spotted and dealt with? If so, surely the fact would have been mentioned. But no, Curran was subtle enough to realise that, once the hope of Hamish was gone, so also was gone any reason for not trying to rush him. The vital question might be just how good a shot was the man at the top of the cliff.

'When you meet your maker,' Curran said conversationally, 'you might just mention that I did warn you. But you failed to heed the warning, and leaving witnesses around is not one of my bad habits. So present my compliments to the Almighty and tell him I sent you.'

The barrel climbed slowly up the short slope of grass and began the ascent of the cliff. The note of the vehicle's engine became louder again. Had Hamish been waiting for extra noise to cover his movement? Keith made up his mind that Hamish was already dead.

Curran was still speaking. 'It was a bit simplistic of you to think that we'd come roaring down with all our lights blazing. Elementary logic suggested that you'd be waiting here if anywhere. In fact, I had a higher opinion of your intelligences. I looked damned carefully before I came down the cliff half a mile away, just in case you'd anticipated me. But no . . .'

Keith braced himself. His tongue rasped dryly against the roof of his mouth. There was a knot in his stomach, and the air in each breath seemed to be spiced with an alien element. He leaned forward slightly, ready for his leap. It might be hopeless, even suicidal, but even that was better than waiting to be blotted out, casually, when Curran took the whim.

At that moment Curran glanced up, checked and looked again. They followed his eyes. A shadow had appeared behind the man at the roadside. One frozen instant passed while life and death were in the balance, and then the man squawked like a seagull and like a gull took off into space. The gun fell in the bushes and fired once, so that a bullet struck a rock and wailed like a cat into the night sky, but the man thumped down on the barrel with a whoosh of expelled breath. The barrel rocked in its sling and the man half-rolled and half-slid into a position between the barrel and the rock wall. Since the barrel was still moving upward Keith had time to think that the man's position was unenviable.

'Sorry I'm late,' Hamish said. 'The bugger kept looking around. Keep those guns pointed at the ground, Curran, or I'll blow you to hell.' The shotgun in his hands glinted.

Curran froze, uncertain of his ability to outshoot Hamish but reluctant to lower his guns and lose his advantage. Hughie Spence, a quicker thinker on the physical plane, dived at Keith in the hope of using him as shelter.

Remembering Cathcart's advice, Keith jumped to meet Spence and swung a blow at the big man's head. He might as well have punched the wall of rock. Keith's fist bounced painfully off the other's skull and he was seized round the waist in a crippling bear-hug and spun round so that he was between Hamish and the big man. But Keith's arms were free and he swung them, short and viciously, so that his hands clapped on the big man's ears. The stunning compression of air inside his head brought Spence to his knees. Keith managed to keep his feet clear. He shook himself free. Ronnie was grabbing up one of the shotguns.

There was no time for thought, yet Keith plucked out of the air the one action that broke the dangerous deadlock. Afterwards, he could not say whether his aim had been to break the 'Mexican standoff' before blood was shed, to save the erstwhile driver who was in immediate danger of being crushed between the barrel and the rock wall, or to put the body of Noddy Chalmers beyond Curran's reach. Whatever his motive, Keith threw himself towards the cliff, plucking as he went the new knife from his belt. He took off from the grass bank as if from a springboard, found two footholds in succession by luck rather than by skill, got one hand on the barrel and somehow dragged himself up onto another foothold, and slashed with his knife at the wire cable.

In an instant, the whole situation disintegrated. The cable parted with a twang like a giant harp. The severed end flashed up, missing Hamish by a hand's breadth, stood vertically above the crane and then fell in festoons around the vehicle.

As the barrel dropped, Keith and the other man fell with it. Keith found himself sitting, half-winded, on the grass bank with his back to the cliff, observing the scene from a grandstand seat. The other man lay unconscious beside him.

The barrel itself had landed on its side on the grass bank. Thrown outward by the initial slope, it set off rolling mightily across the level ground towards the brink of the sloping farm-land, shedding the tail of the cable and the last of its staves as it went.

Curran saw the barrel-shaped ice-block coming. His first instinct was to stop it departing forever over the brink. He took a step to the side and braced himself to take the shock. At the last moment he must have realised that he could no more stop that trundling mass than a daffodil could withstand a garden roller. Too late to leap to either side, he went in the only direction still open to him, which was straight up in a standing high-jump that any circus performer might have envied. High as it was, it was not high enough. The mass of ice, as it passed below, took his feet with it. Curran came down from a height, flat on his face on the frozen ground. The two guns skittered out of his hands. Cathcart pounced immediately, one hand already fishing for his handcuffs.

The ice-barrel, quite unconcerned about these human antics, bore its dead burden right to the edge of the slope. There, at the mouth of the lane, it found the depression made by the passage of people for a hundred years and it lurched into an upright position, oscillating on its base. Keith, spellbound, was treated to his last view of Noddy Chalmers against the glow of the town's lights, a misty shape squatting Buddha-like in his block of ice. Black flowers seemed to be growing from his chest. For a second or two it seemed that Noddy was taking a last look around; then the rim went over the edge, the ice-block toppled, rolled and entered the mouth of the track. Without being aware of moving, Keith found himself standing at the top of the slope, watching it go. Twice it slewed, tried to climb the bank, failed and set off again. Then it settled into steady progress and accelerated heavily.

Keith glanced round, and jumped when he found Hughie Spence beside him. But the big man had accepted the situation philosophically; with no fee in view, he saw no reason to take further action. He was looking with dour amusement down the hill. 'Your car?' he asked.

Helped by a drop in ground-level, the ice-roller hesitated at Keith's car and passed on. The car, which had already been low to the ground, now hardly made a hump in the lane.

'It was,' Keith said sadly, for he had enjoyed the little car. And he had refused to sell it to Janet.

'Tough!' The big man held out his hand. 'No hard feelings?'

Keith took the hand, and his own was held in the feather-light grip peculiar to the very strong. Only later did he think what an extraordinary gesture that handshake was.

'I'll away then,' Spence said. He looked at Cathcart and then up at Hamish. His big form flitted away into the shadows.

Inspector Cathcart was fully occupied. Seated comfortably on Archie Curran's shoulder-blades, he was speaking to the handcuffed man in low tones and at the same time rubbing the man's face to and fro on the icy ground. With his toe, Keith flicked Curran's automatic into the bushes. He could recover it later, and Hughie Spence could take the blame for its disappearance.

Ronnie, unusually silent, had joined Keith. Together they looked down the long hill. Noddy Chalmers was still travelling in a straight line. He knew exactly where he was going, and for once in his existence he was going there of his own accord.

SIXTEEN

'There's no doubt at all about the gems,' Andrew Gulliver said. 'They correspond exactly with the missing stones and you were responsible for the recovery. You'll get your pound of flesh.'

'And the reward on the money?' Keith asked.

Gulliver shrugged. 'When a number of sums of money have been moved from account to account and then turned into cash, how do you prove that the cash is still the same money? I think we'll prove it in the end and you'll get the reward. But it's going to take a year or two, and I suspect that the lawyers will make more out of it than any of us will. But then, they usually do.'

Keith signalled to the barmaid for another couple of drinks. 'Would you really have taken me to court if I'd blown it?'

Gulliver looked surprised. 'If it could have been proved that recovery was prevented because you'd kept a vital piece of evidence to yourself, yes, of course I would. That's the name of the game. You took a piece of the action in the hope of a reward, so you also took the risk of action against you if you were counter-productive. I wasn't against you, mind. I was hoping you'd pull it off. But I had to warn you.'

'I didn't believe you,' Keith said.

'More fool you.'

'Keith?' said Ronnie's voice over the phone. 'I swear I didn't mean to drop you in the clag.'

'What have you done now?' Keith demanded.

'Where's Molly?'

'Away up to see Sir Peter.'

'Christ! That's where Janet's heading.'

'What, if anything, are you havering about?' Keith said. 'What have you done?'

'Och, it was too good a story not to tell. I telled Janet about you and yon lassie of Danny Bruce's, you being alone together and her hog-tied and all.'

'Are you bloody dottled?' Keith paused and regained control of his voice. 'What did you want to go and tell the lassie a thing like that for.'

'I told her in confidence,' Ronnie said defensively. 'But then I saw from the look in her eye that she was out to make mischief and I thought I'd better call you. I thought maybe you could head her off.'

'You head her off,' Keith said. 'If I try to stop Janet, Molly'll not believe it was just you shooting your stupid mouth off as usual. And you're nearer. You'd better head her off quick. If this gets back to Molly, I'll load you full of Nobel Eighty and touch it off.'

' – and Ronnie said that they were alone together for more than half an hour,' Janet said triumphantly. 'Doesn't just the thought of it make you go all shivery?'

It did, but Molly had no intention of saying as much to anyone, and least of all to Janet. 'If that's your idea of a good time,' she said coldly, 'Ronnie might oblige.'

When Molly married Keith she had known him for a philanderer, but she had loved him and had preferred the chance of happiness to the certainty of grief. In the ensuing months, Keith's fidelity had pleased her deeply, but she knew that the habits might have changed but not the man and that some day she would have to face some lapse that she could not ignore. Keith had at least given her time to consider what her attitude would be, and she had decided firmly against making herself less attractive by displaying anger or hurt. Instead, Keith must realise that his wife had at least as much to offer as other women; and if he still craved the stimulus of variety he must go out into the world too spent to respond to it.

Molly hurried home. While her bath ran, she produced from a deep drawer her most outrageous lingerie. She took some thick steaks from the freezer and a bottle of rich, red wine from under the stairs. A touch of jealousy would do Keith no harm, and after a mental review of suitable bachelors she settled on Inspector Cathcart.

Keith was due for the full treatment.

Unaware of what was in store for him, Keith was out looking for his brother-in-law. His search was unsuccessful, for Ronnie was making himself very scarce. He could quite believe that Keith would be carrying with him a tin of Smokeless Powder, and would use it exactly as he had threatened.

'Mr Ledbetter? Keith Calder here. Can you tell me when our estate-car's going to be ready?'

Mr Ledbetter hesitated. In the background Keith could hear Sir Peter's voice, arguing with the mechanic over repairs to a tractor. 'A whilie yet,' said Mr Ledbetter.

'Do you have another car you could let me have on hire?'

'Aye, I do. But what's adae with the wee sports car?'

'You haven't heard? I thought it was all over the town.'

'I've been away,' said Mr Ledbetter.

Keith sighed. 'I'm not sure you're going to believe this,' he began.